ONE DAY AT HORRORLAND

Look for more Goosebumps books
by R.L. Stine:

Goosebumps

ONE DAY AT HORRORLAND

R.L. STINE

AN
APPLE
PAPERBACK

SCHOLASTIC INC.
New York Toronto London Auckland Sydney

ISBN 0-590-47738-2

25 24 23 22 21 20   5 6 7 8 9/9

Printed in the U.S.A.   40

First Scholastic printing, February 1994

1

As we entered the gates to HorrorLand, we had no idea that, in less than an hour, we would all be lying in our coffins.

I'm the calm one in the Morris family. Everyone says, "Lizzy, you're the calm one." And I'm trying to tell this story calmly.

But, believe me — there's *no way*!

We had never planned to go to HorrorLand. In fact, we'd never heard of it.

The five of us were squeezed into Dad's little Toyota, on our way to spend the day at Zoo Gardens Theme Park. Dad had messed up and left the map at home. But Mom said the park would be real easy to find.

When we got close to the park, Mom said, there would be lots of signs to direct us. But so far we hadn't seen a single sign.

Dad was driving, and Mom was beside him in the front. I was squeezed in back with my little brother Luke, who is ten, and Luke's friend Clay.

It wasn't the best place to be. My brother cannot sit still for a second. Especially in the car. He just has too much energy. And he's totally goofy.

The longer we drove, the more restless Luke became. He tried wrestling with Clay, but there really wasn't room. Then he tried arm wrestling with him, and the two of them kept bumping me until I lost my temper and started shouting at them to stop.

"Why don't you three play Alphabets?" Mom suggested from the front. "Look out the window for letters."

"There aren't any," Luke replied. "There aren't any signs."

"There isn't *anything* to look at," Clay grumbled.

He was right. We were driving past flat, sandy fields. There were a few scraggly trees here and there. The rest was all desert.

"I'm going to take this turnoff," Dad announced. He took off his Chicago Cubs cap and scratched his thinning blond hair. "Haven't I already taken this turnoff?"

Dad is the only blond in the family. Mom, Luke, and I all have straight black hair and blue eyes.

In fact, Dad doesn't look as if he belongs in the same family. The three of us are tall and thin, with very fair skin. And Dad is short and kind of chubby, with a round face that's almost always pink. I tease him all the time because I think he looks a lot more like a wrestler than a bank manager, which he is.

"I'm pretty sure we've already been here," Dad said unhappily.

"It's hard to tell. It's all desert," Mom replied, gazing out her window.

"Very helpful," Dad muttered.

"How can I be helpful?" Mom shot back. "*You're* the one who left the map on the kitchen table."

"I thought you packed it," Dad grumbled.

"Why should it be my job to pack the map?" Mom cried.

"Break it up, you two," I interrupted. Once they start fighting, they never stop. It's always best to interrupt them quickly before they really get into it.

"I'm the Mad Pincher!" Luke cried. He let out a gruesome, horror-movie laugh and started pinching Clay's ribs and arms.

I hate Luke's Mad Pincher routine more than anything. I was so glad that Clay was sitting in the middle next to Luke, and not me. Usually, the only way to stop Luke's pinching is to slug him.

Clay started squirming and laughing. He thinks everything Luke does is a riot. He laughs at all of my brother's stupid jokes and stunts. I think that's why Luke likes Clay so much.

The two of them began pinching each other. Then Luke shoved Clay onto me. "Give me a break!" I cried.

I shoved Clay back. I know I shouldn't have. But it was getting hot in the car, and we'd been driving for hours, and what was I supposed to do?

"Lizzy! Boys! Chill out back there!" Dad cried.

"Dad, nobody says 'chill out' anymore," I told him calmly and quietly.

For some reason, that made him go berserk. He started yelling, and his face got bright red.

I knew he wasn't mad at me. He was mad because he couldn't find Zoo Gardens Theme Park.

"Everybody just take a deep breath and be silent," Mom suggested.

"Ow! Stop pinching me!" Clay screamed. He gave Luke a hard shove.

"*You* stop pinching *me!*" my brother shrieked, shoving him back.

Boys can really be animals.

"Hey, look — a sign up ahead!" Mom pointed as a large green sign came into view.

Luke and Clay stopped fighting. Dad leaned forward over the steering wheel, squinting through the windshield.

"Does it say where the park is?" Luke demanded.

"Does it say where we are?" Clay asked.

The words on the sign came into view as we

4

drove past it. It said: SIGN FOR RENT.

We all let out disappointed groans.

"The Mad Pincher returns!" Luke cried. He gave Clay a hard pinch on the arm. Luke never knows when to quit.

"This road isn't going anywhere," Dad said, scowling. "I'll have to turn around and get back on the highway. If I can find it."

"I think you should ask someone for directions," Mom suggested.

"Ask someone? Ask someone?" Dad exploded. "Do you *see* anyone I can ask?" His face was bright red again. He drove with one hand so he could use the other to shake a fist.

"I meant if you see a gas station," Mom murmured.

"A gas station?" Dad screamed. "I don't even see a tree!"

Dad was right. I stared out the window and saw nothing but white sand on both sides of the road. The sun beamed down on it, making it gleam. The sand was so bright, it nearly looked like snow.

"I meant to go north," Dad muttered. "The desert is south. We must have gone south."

"You'd better turn around," Mom urged.

"Are we lost?" Clay asked. I could hear some fear in his voice.

Clay isn't the bravest kid in the world. In fact, he is pretty easy to scare. Once I crept up behind him in our back yard at night and whispered his name — and he almost jumped right out of his shoes!

"Dad, are we lost?" Luke repeated the question.

"Yeah, we're lost," Dad replied quietly. "Hopelessly lost."

Clay let out a soft cry and slumped in the seat. He looked a little like a balloon deflating.

"Don't tell him that!" Mom cried sharply.

"What *should* I tell him?" Dad snapped back. "We're nowhere near Zoo Gardens. We're nowhere near civilization! We're in the desert, going nowhere!"

"Just turn around. I'm sure we'll find someone we can ask," Mom said softly. "And stop being so dramatic."

"We're all going to die in the desert," Luke said, with a gruesome grin on his face. "And buzzards will peck out our eyeballs and eat our flesh."

My brother has a great sense of humor, doesn't he?

You can't imagine what it's like having to live with a total ghoul!

"Luke, stop scaring Clay," Mom said, turning in her seat to glare at Luke.

"I'm not scared," Clay insisted. But he looked scared. His round face was kind of pale. And his eyes were blinking a lot behind his glasses. With his short, feathery blond hair and round eyeglasses, Clay looked a lot like a frightened owl.

Muttering to himself, Dad slowed the car to a stop. Then he turned it around, and we headed back in the direction we had come. "Great vacation," he said through clenched teeth.

"It's still early," Mom told him, checking her watch.

The late morning sun was nearly straight overhead. I could feel its warmth on my face through the open sunroof.

We drove for nearly half an hour. Luke wanted to play Twenty Questions or Geography with Clay. But Clay moodily said no. He just stared out the window, watching the desert roll by. Every few minutes, he'd ask, "Are we still lost?"

"Pretty lost," my dad would reply unhappily.

"We're okay," Mom kept reassuring us.

As we drove, the scraggly trees reappeared. Then, after a while, the sand gave way to darker fields, dotted with trees and low shrubs.

I sat silently, my hands clasped in my lap, staring out the window. I wasn't really scared or worried. But I wished we would at least see a gas station or a store or one other human being!

"I'm getting hungry," Luke griped. "Is it lunchtime?"

With a long sigh that sounded like air escaping from a tire, Dad pulled the car to the side of the road. He reached across Mom to the glove compartment. "There's *got* to be some kind of map in there," he said.

7

"No. I already looked," Mom told him.

As they started to argue, I raised my eyes to the open sunroof above my head.

"Oh!" I let out a cry as I saw a hideous monster staring down at me, lowering its enormous head, about to crush the car.

I opened my mouth to scream, but no sound came out.

The monster glared down at me through the sunroof. It was as tall as a building, I realized. Its red eyes glowed with evil, and its mouth was twisted in a hungry grin.

"D-Dad!" I finally managed to stammer. Dad was bent over, fumbling through the papers in the glove compartment.

"Wow!" I heard Luke cry.

I turned and saw that Luke was staring up at it, too, his blue eyes wide with fright.

"Dad? Mom?" My heart was pounding so hard, I thought my chest might explode.

"Lizzy, what is it?" Mom asked impatiently.

The monster lowered its head over us. Its mouth opened wide, ready to swallow the whole car.

And then Luke started to laugh. "Wow! Cool!" he cried.

9

And I realized at the same time that the monster wasn't alive. It was a mechanical figure, part of a giant billboard display.

Ducking my head to get a better view through the side window, I saw that Dad had pulled the car up right beside the billboard. My parents were so busy arguing about maps, they hadn't even noticed it!

I stared up at the red-eyed monster. It lowered its head and opened its jaws. Then the jaws snapped shut, and the enormous head slid back up.

"It looks so real!" Clay exclaimed, staring up at it.

"Didn't fool me," I lied. I wasn't going to admit that I nearly leaped out through the sunroof. I'm supposed to be the calm one, after all.

I rolled down the window and stuck my head out to read the billboard in front of the mechanical monster. In huge red letters it said: WELCOME TO HORRORLAND WHERE NIGHTMARES COME TO LIFE!

There was a dark red arrow in the upper left-hand corner, with the words: ONE MILE.

"Can we go there?" Luke demanded eagerly. He leaned forward and grabbed the back of Dad's seat with both hands. "Can we, Dad? How about it?"

"It looks kind of scary," Clay said softly.

Dad slammed the glove compartment shut with

a sigh. He was giving up on the map idea. "Luke, stop pulling my seat," he snapped. "Sit back."

"Can we go to HorrorLand?" Luke demanded.

"HorrorLand? What's HorrorLand?" Mom demanded.

"Never heard of it," Dad muttered.

"It's only a mile from here," Luke pleaded. "It looks great!"

The monster lowered its head over the car, staring in through the sunroof. Then it raised its head again.

"I don't think so," Mom said, staring out at the huge billboard. "Zoo Gardens is such a wonderful park. HorrorLand doesn't look very nice."

"It looks great!" Luke insisted, pulling at Dad's seat back again. "It looks really excellent!"

"Luke, sit back," Dad pleaded.

"Let's go," I urged. "We're never going to find Zoo Gardens."

Mom hesitated, chewing her lower lip. "I don't know," she said fretfully. "Some of these places aren't safe."

"It'll be safe!" Luke declared. "It'll be very safe!"

"Luke — sit back!" Dad growled.

"Can we go?" Luke demanded, ignoring Dad's request. "Can we?"

"It could be fun," Clay said quietly.

"Let's give it a try," I urged them. "If we hate it, we can always leave."

Dad rubbed his chin. He sighed. "Well, I guess it would be better than sitting here in the middle of nowhere arguing all day."

"YAAAAAY!" Luke screamed.

Luke and I reached over Clay to slap each other a high five. HorrorLand sounded like a pretty cool place to me, too. I love scary rides.

"If the rides are as scary as that monster," I said, pointing at the billboard, "this park will be awesome!"

"You don't think it's *too* scary — do you?" Clay asked. I saw that he had his hands clasped tightly in his lap. And he had that frightened owl look on his face again.

"No, it won't be *too* scary," I told him.

Oh, wow — was I *wrong*!

"I can't believe someone would build a big theme park out in the wilderness," Dad declared.

We were driving through what seemed like an endless forest. Tall, old trees leaned over the two-lane road, nearly blocking out the late morning sun.

"Maybe they haven't built the park yet," Mom suggested. "Maybe they're going to clear out these trees and build the park here."

All three of us in the back seat were hoping Mom was wrong. And she was.

The road curved sharply. And as we came out

of the curve, we saw the tall gates to the park straight up ahead.

Behind a tall, purple fence, HorrorLand seemed to stretch for miles. Leaning forward in my seat, I could see the tops of rides and strange, colorful buildings. As we drove across the enormous parking lot, eerie chords of organ music invaded the car.

"YAAAAAY! This looks *great!*" Luke exclaimed.

Clay and I enthusiastically agreed. I couldn't wait to get out of the car and see everything.

"The parking lot is nearly empty," Dad said, glancing uneasily at Mom.

"That means we won't have to wait in long lines!" I quickly exclaimed.

"I think Lizzy is excited about this place," Mom commented, smiling.

"Me, too!" Luke cried. He punched Clay enthusiastically on the shoulder. Luke always has to be punching or pinching somebody.

We crossed the wide parking lot. I saw a few cars parked near the front gate. At the far side of the lot stood a row of purple-and-green buses with the word *HorrorLand* across the side.

As we rode closer, I got a good look at the front gate. The same monster we had seen behind the billboard rose up behind a big purple-and-green sign over the gate. The sign read: *THE*

HORRORLAND HORRORS WELCOME YOU TO
HORRORLAND!

"I don't *get* that sign," Mom said. "What are
the HorrorLand Horrors?"

"We'll find out!" I exclaimed happily.

The solemn, eerie organ music floated heavily
over the parking lot. Dad pulled into a space in
an empty aisle to the right of the front gate.

Luke and I pushed open the back doors before
the car had even stopped. "Let's go!" I cried.

Luke, Clay, and I started trotting toward the
gate. As I ran, I stared up at the green monster
over the sign. This one didn't move its head like
the billboard monster. But it looked very real.

I glanced back and saw that Mom and Dad were
hurrying to catch up with us. "This is going to be
way cool!" I exclaimed.

And then I gasped as a deafening explosion
made the ground shake.

And I stared back in horror as our car burst
apart, exploding into a million pieces.

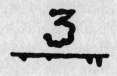

It took me a long while to stop screaming. Finally, I swallowed hard, choking back my cries.

We all stared in shock. Small chunks of twisted metal and a few burning cinders were all that was left of our car.

"How — ?" was all Dad managed to say.

"I — I d-don't believe it!" I stammered.

"Thank goodness we were all out of the car!" Mom cried. She gathered us up in a big hug. "Thank goodness we're all okay."

Luke and Clay still hadn't uttered a sound. They stood wide-eyed, staring at the spot where the car had stood.

"My car!" Dad choked out in a horrified whisper. "My car . . . How? How?"

"We're safe," Mom murmured. "We're all safe. What a terrifying explosion. I can't get the sound of it out of my ears."

"I — I've got to call the police!" Dad sputtered.

He began trotting to the gate, shaking his head, muttering to himself.

"How could the car just blow up like that, dear?" Mom asked, hurrying after him. "What would make it *do* that?"

"How should I know?" Dad snapped angrily. "I — I don't get it! I really don't! And *now* what are we going to do?" He sounded really panicked.

I didn't blame him. The explosion was really scary.

And when I realized that we could have all been inside the car when it went off, I had cold chills down my back.

"Maybe there's a rental car place we can call," Mom suggested.

Mom is like me, calm in any emergency.

We followed Dad as he went running up to the ticket booth at the entrance. A green monster stood in the booth. He had bulging yellow eyes, and dark horns curled over his head. It was a really great costume.

"Welcome to HorrorLand," he said in a gruff, low voice. A loud stab of organ music rose up from inside the ticket booth. "I am a HorrorLand Horror. All of the Horrors and I hope you have a scary day."

"My car!" Dad cried frantically. "There was an explosion. I need a phone!"

"I'm sorry, sir. No phones," the guy in the monster costume replied.

16

"Huh?" Dad's face was bright red again. His forehead was drenched with sweat. "But I *need* a phone! Right away!" Dad insisted, glaring angrily at the green monster. "My car exploded! We're stuck here!"

"We'll take care of you," the Horror replied, lowering his gruff voice nearly to a whisper.

"You'll *what*?" Dad cried. "We need a car. I need to get to a phone! Don't you understand?"

"No phones," the monster repeated. "But, please, sir. Allow us to take care of you. I promise we will take care of everything. Don't let this spoil your visit to HorrorLand."

"Spoil my visit?!" Dad shrieked, his face growing even redder. "But my car — !"

Another loud stab of organ music made me jump. The creepy music made me feel as if I were actually in a horror movie!

"We will take care of you. I promise," the Horror said. A strange smile crossed his face. His yellow eyes lit up. "Please enjoy your stay, and do not worry about transportation. The other Horrors and I will see that you are properly taken care of."

"But — but — " Dad sputtered.

The Horror gestured toward the park. "Please enter as our guests. Free admission. I apologize for your car. But, please, do not worry. I promise you will have no need to worry about your car."

Dad turned back to us, sweat dripping down

17

his forehead. I could see that he was really upset. "I — I can't enjoy an amusement park now," he said. "I can't believe this happened. I really can't. We've got to get a car somehow, and — "

"Oh, please, Dad!" Luke cried. "Please! Can't we go inside? He said he'll take care of it for us."

"Just for a little while?" I joined my brother in pleading.

"We've had such a long drive," Mom told Dad. "Let's go in for a short while. Let them blow off some steam."

Dad thought about it, frowning hard. "Okay. Just for a little while," he agreed finally.

The organ music grew louder as we stepped through the gate. "Wow! Look at this place!" I cried. "It really is like being in a horror movie."

We were standing on a brown, cobbled street. Strange, dark cottages tilted up on both sides of the street. Tall trees along the street nearly blocked out all the sunlight. The air carried a chill.

Low howls, like wolf howls, floated out from the cottages.

"Cool!" Luke declared.

A sign proclaimed: WELCOME TO WERE-WOLF VILLAGE. DO NOT FEED THE WERE-WOLVES. IF YOU CAN HELP IT.

The frightening howls grew louder.

Luke and I laughed at the sign.

I saw a green monster, one of the Horrors, staring out at us through a dark window in the

18

cottage across the narrow street. Another Horror walked past carrying a very real-looking human head. He grasped it by its long, blond hair and bounced it up and down, sort of like a yo-yo, as he walked.

"Cool!" Luke proclaimed again. It seemed to be his word of the day.

We walked along the cobbled street. The sound of our thudding sneakers echoed off the cottage walls.

"Ohh!" We all let out cries of surprise as a long, low, gray wolf ran in front of us. It disappeared around the side of a cottage before we really got a good look at it.

"Was that a real wolf?" Clay asked, his voice shaking.

"Of course not," I told him. "It was probably a dog. Or else it was mechanical."

"Well, they certainly keep this park clean," Mom said, trying to sound cheerful. "There isn't a piece of trash or dirt anywhere. Of course, it isn't very crowded."

Dad lingered behind. "I — I've got to find a phone," he said fretfully. "I can't enjoy this until I know we have a way to get home."

"But, dear — " Mom started.

"There's got to be a phone somewhere," Dad interrupted. "Go on without me."

"No. I'll come with you," Mom said. "You're in such a frantic state. You'll need me to make the calls for you. The kids will have a better time without us hanging around anyway."

"Leave them?" Dad cried. "You mean, let them go on their own?"

"Of course," Mom said, hurrying back to him. "They'll be perfectly fine. This looks like a very nice place. What could happen?"

What could happen?

With those words, Mom and Dad rushed off to find a phone.

"Meet back here!" Mom called to us.

Luke, Clay, and I were suddenly on our own.

I turned to watch Mom and Dad hurry away.

I turned back in time to see a gray wolf edging out from behind the cottage. It lowered its head and let out a rumbling warning growl.

All three of us froze as we realized its hungry red eyes were locked on us.

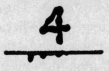

I cried out and pulled Luke and Clay back.

The wolf slithered out, holding its head low, glaring up at us with wide red eyes, its mouth open hungrily.

"It — it's real!" Clay declared, swallowing hard. I had my hand on his shoulder. I could feel him trembling.

The wolf let out a low growl.

Then it slid back behind the cottage wall.

"I think it's some kind of robot or something," I told Clay.

"Let's go somewhere else," Clay replied, suddenly very pale.

"What does that sign up there say?" Luke asked. He went running over the dark cobblestones to the sign, and Clay and I followed.

The sign read: *No Pinching.*

Luke laughed. "That's stupid."

"What a dumb sign!" Clay agreed.

"That sign was meant just for you, Luke!" I

exclaimed. I gave him a hard pinch on the arm.

"Hey! Can't you read?" he shouted angrily, pointing to the sign.

I saw a green Horror watching us from down the street. Then I saw a family making its way behind the row of cottages. There was a mother, a father, and a little girl. The little girl was crying, for some reason. The parents had their hands on her shoulders and looked very upset.

A wolf howl cut through the air.

"Let's find some rides!" Clay suggested.

"Some *scary* rides!" Luke added.

Walking side by side, keeping close together, we made our way out of the Werewolf Village. The street widened into a round plaza. Bright sunlight returned as soon as we stepped out of the village.

Several purple-and-green buildings surrounded the plaza. I saw a few more families and several green-costumed Horrors keeping an eye on everything. A pudgy Horror behind a purple-and-green cart was selling ice cream cones — *black* ice cream!

"Yuck!" Luke declared, making a face.

We hurried past the cart, past another *No Pinching* sign, and stopped in front of what appeared to be a tall purple mountain.

"It's a ride!" I told them.

A doorway was cut into the side of the mountain. And above the doorway was a sign: *DOOM*

*SLIDE. WILL YOU BE THE ONE TO SLIDE
FOREVER?*

"Cool!" Luke cried, slapping Clay a high five.

"I'll bet you climb to the top, then slide all the
way down," I said, pointing to the top of the
mountain-shaped building.

"Let's go!" Luke cried excitedly.

We ran to the building, then through the open
doorway in its side. It was dark and cold inside.
A wide ramp curved up toward the top.

I could hear kids squealing and laughing, but I
couldn't see them. The three of us half-walked,
half-ran up the ramp, eager to get to the top.

About halfway up, we stopped to read another
sign: *WARNING! — YOU MAY BE THE ONE TO
SLIDE TO YOUR DOOM!*

Now I could hear kids screaming as they slid
down. But it was too dark to see anything. "Are
you scared, Clay?" I asked, noticing his tight expression.

"No way!" he insisted, embarrassed by my
question. "I've seen these things before. They're
like really huge sliding boards. You just sit on
them and slide down."

"Hurry!" Luke shouted, running ahead of us.

"Hey — wait up!" I called. I followed them to
the top of the ramp. We found ourselves on a wide
platform. A row of long, curving sliding boards
stretched to the end of the platform. The sliding
boards were numbered from one to ten.

In the dim light, I saw two Horrors watching us approach. They stood in front of the sliding boards. Their bulging yellow eyes lit up as we hurried over to them.

"Do you slide all the way down?" Luke asked one of them.

The Horror nodded.

"Do you go really fast?" Clay asked, lingering a few feet behind us.

The Horror nodded again. "It's a long way down," he rumbled.

"Be careful which slide you pick," the other Horror warned. "Don't pick the Doom Slide." He gestured to the number painted in black in front of each slide.

"Yes. Don't pick the Doom Slide," his partner repeated. "You'll slide down forever and ever."

I laughed.

He was just trying to scare us — *wasn't* he?

5

I chose slide number three because three is my lucky number. Luke sat down on top of the slide next to mine, slide number two. And Clay scrambled over to the far end and dropped down onto slide number ten.

I glanced back to see what the Horrors were doing. But before I could focus on them, I felt the bottom tilt underneath me.

I let out a long, high-pitched shriek as I began to slide.

I raised my arms over my head, leaned back, and screamed all the way down. My cries echoed in the enormous, dark canyon of the Doom Slide building.

It felt great. The slide curved and curved, and I swirled down in the darkness, faster and faster.

In the shadowy light, I could see Luke in the slide next to mine. He was lying on his back, staring straight up with his mouth wide open.

I tried to call out to him. But the slide curved away, and I curved with it.

Down, down.

I was sliding so fast, the darkness became a solid blur.

The slide curved up, then around, then down again. I'm a human roller coaster, I thought happily.

Down, down. Darker and darker.

I'm sliding faster than the speed of light, I thought.

I glanced from one side to the other, trying to see Luke and Clay. But it was too dark, and I was moving too fast.

Too fast.

And, then, *bump*.

A chute opened up. I hit the ground hard, landing on the seat of my jeans.

Outside. I was back outside.

Bump.

Luke bounced out beside me. He hit the ground, still lying on his back, and made no attempt to get up. He grinned up at me. "Where am I?"

"Back on the ground," I told him, climbing to my feet. I brushed off the back of my jeans, then reached behind my head to straighten my braid. "Great ride, huh?"

"Let's go again," Luke said, still lying there.

"We can't go again if you don't get up," I said.

"Help me." He reached up a hand.

I groaned as I tugged him to a sitting position. "Get up yourself," I said impatiently.

"You were screaming in there," he told me.

"I did it on purpose," I said. "I *wanted* to scream."

"Yeah. Sure." He rolled his eyes. Then he pulled himself to his feet. "Wow. I'm a little dizzy. How fast do you think we were going?"

I shrugged. "Pretty fast, I think. It's so dark in there, it's hard to know how fast you're going."

And then I realized we were missing a member of our sliding party. I stared at the closed chutes on the wall of the building. "Hey — where's Clay?"

"Huh?" Luke had forgotten about him, too.

We both stared at the side of the building, waiting for Clay to pop out.

"Where is he?" Luke demanded shrilly. "He couldn't be that much slower than us — could he?"

I shook my head. I was starting to feel really nervous. I had a heavy feeling in the pit of my stomach. And my hands were suddenly cold and clammy.

"Come on, Clay," I pleaded, staring at the wall. "Come on out."

Luke scratched his black hair. "Where'd he go?" he asked. "Why didn't Clay come out?"

"Maybe he came out the front," I said. "Maybe slide number ten dumps you out in front. Let's check it out."

As we ran around the building toward the front, I scolded myself for getting scared so easily. Of *course* Clay came out in a different chute. He was probably waiting for us in front of the building. He was probably worried about *us*.

As we rounded the purple building, the wide, circular plaza came into view. I searched for Mom and Dad, but they weren't there. I saw a couple of other families on the other side of the circle, and the pudgy green Horror leaning on his ice-cream cart.

No sign of Clay.

Luke and I kept running, up to the front entrance of the Doom Slide. We stopped a few feet from the dark opening.

"He isn't here!" Luke cried, struggling to catch his breath.

I was breathing hard, too. And the heavy feeling of dread in my stomach grew even heavier. "No. No Clay," I muttered.

"What are we going to do?" Luke asked. His blue eyes were wide with fear.

I saw a green Horror woman standing just inside the entrance. "Hey!" I called as I ran over to her. "Did you see a kid come out of there?" I asked breathlessly.

The yellow eyes on the Horror's mask bulged and appeared to light up. "No. This is the entrance. No one comes out here," she replied.

"He's blond and sort of chubby. He wears

glasses," I told her. "He's wearing a blue T-shirt and denim shorts."

The Horror shook her head. "No. No one comes out this way. Did you check the back? Everyone comes out the back."

"He didn't!" Luke said shrilly. "We were there. He didn't come out." My brother's voice came out high and squeaky. He was breathing so hard, his chest was heaving up and down. He was in a panic.

I was frightened, too. But I knew I had to stay calm. For Luke's sake.

"He didn't come out the back," I told the Horror, "and he didn't come out the front. So what happened to him?"

The Horror was silent for a long moment. Then she said in a low voice just above a whisper, "Maybe your friend chose the Doom Slide."

6

I stared at the woman in the Horror costume. "You — you're joking, right?" I stammered. "I mean, the Doom Slide — that's just a joke."

She stared back with her bulging yellow eyes and didn't reply. "The signs give a warning," she said. "There's always a warning."

She turned and disappeared into the dark entrance. Luke and I goggled at each other. I swallowed hard. My throat suddenly felt very dry. My hands were cold as ice now.

"This is stupid," Luke muttered. He jammed his hands into his jeans pockets. "It's just a dumb slide. Why is she trying to scare us?"

"I guess that's her job," I told him.

"We've got to find Mom and Dad," Luke muttered.

"We've got to find Clay first," I told him. "If Mom and Dad find out we lost Clay, they'll get angry and make us go home as soon as we find him."

"*If* we find him," Luke said glumly.

I glanced back across the plaza. No Mom and Dad. Two teenagers were buying black ice-cream cones from the Horror at the cart. Two Horrors were sweeping the plaza with push brooms, working side by side.

Far in the distance, I could hear the howl of a wolf from the Werewolf Village.

The sun was high in the sky now. I could feel it beaming down on top of my head and on my shoulders. But I still felt cold all over.

"Clay — where *are* you?" I asked, thinking out loud.

"He's sliding forever," Luke said, shaking his head. "Sliding forever and ever on the Doom Slide."

"That's dumb," I replied. But Luke had given me an idea. "Come on," I said, tugging the sleeve of his T-shirt. I started pulling him to the dark entrance.

"Huh? Where?" Luke pulled back.

"We'll go on the slides again," I told him.

His mouth dropped open in protest. "Without Clay? We can't go on it again without Clay."

"We're going to find Clay," I said, grabbing his arm this time and pulling him to the dark, open doorway.

"You mean — ?" My brother was starting to catch on.

I nodded. "Yes. We'll follow him. We'll take the same slide he took."

"Slide number ten," Luke murmured. And then he added in a solemn whisper, "The Doom Slide."

"We'll take it, and it will lead us right to him," I said.

We climbed the ramp in silence. The rapid *thud* of our sneakers echoed in the vast, hollow mountain.

We ran past the sign about halfway up to the top. I read it again as I passed it by: *WARNING! YOU MAY BE THE ONE TO SLIDE TO YOUR DOOM!*

Clay — are you still sliding? I wondered.

I shook my head hard, shaking away the thought. Of *course* he wasn't still sliding. What a stupid idea!

The two Horrors were still standing at the top of the slides. "Be careful which slide you pick," one of them warned.

"We know which one we want," I said breathlessly. "Slide number ten. Both of us. Together."

The Horror nearest the slide motioned for us to sit down. I glanced at Luke, who stood right behind me, his features tight with fear.

He tugged me back a few steps. "Maybe we shouldn't," he whispered.

"Why not?" I demanded impatiently.

"What if the warning is *true*?" Luke demanded.

"Don't be dumb," I scolded him. "This is an amusement park — remember? They don't kill

32

kids or send them sliding to their doom. It's all for fun!"

Luke swallowed hard. "You sure?"

"Of course I'm sure," I replied. "Now do you want to find Clay or not?"

Luke nodded.

"Then let's go," I ordered.

I sat down at the top of slide number ten. Luke plopped down right behind me, stretching his legs outside of mine.

I felt the floor tilt up beneath us.

We started to slide.

"Clay, here we come!" I cried.

7

I didn't scream this time. I clasped my hands in my lap and gritted my teeth.

There was no way I was going to enjoy this ride. I just wanted to get to the end of it. I wanted to solve the mystery and find Clay.

As we slid down together, Luke grabbed onto me, his hands gripping my waist. He cried out when we slid over a big bump, and it felt as if we were going to go flying off the slide.

Then we both screamed as the slide took a steep dive — almost straight down — and we started to fall.

We landed hard, and then the slide curved sharply to the right. We were both screaming our lungs out now.

We were sliding faster and faster, in total darkness, blacker than black. I tried to see if we were moving alongside the other slides. But it was so dark, I couldn't even see my sneakers in front of me!

Luke squeezed my waist so hard, I could hardly breathe. I tried to tell him to loosen his grip, but he was screaming too loud to hear.

Down, down.

Darker and darker.

We hit another bump that sent us bouncing up into the air. Then the slide dipped and curved sharply to the left.

We should be at the bottom by now, I realized.

We'd been sliding a very long time.

I gritted my teeth harder and tried to brace myself to go flying out the chute and bumping onto the ground.

But no chute opened.

The ride didn't end.

We began to slide faster. I gasped in mouthfuls of the hot, damp air, struggling to catch my breath.

The slide dipped and curved, sending us down into the thick, heavy blackness.

We're going to slide forever.

The warning sign didn't lie.

I struggled to force those frightening thoughts from my mind.

Luke suddenly got very quiet. "Are you okay?" I called back to him.

"I don't know," he replied, holding on even tighter. "Why are we sliding so long?"

"You're *hurting* me!" I cried.

He loosened his hold a little. "I don't like this!" he shouted in my ear.

We hit another bump. His hands flew off me.

Another bump. Even harder. I thought I was going to fly off the slide and fall to the bottom — if there *was* a bottom.

Down, down.

Luke and I both cried out in disgust as something sticky covered our faces. I reached up with both hands and tried to pull it off.

"Yuck!" Luke screamed. "What *is* it? My face — !"

"It's like cobwebs," I shouted back at him. "Hot, sticky cobwebs."

My whole face itched. The sticky threads covered my face like a net. I pulled frantically at them.

"Oh!" I cried out as the slide took another sharp dip.

Tearing at the sticky cobwebs, I managed to pull most of them off. But my face still itched like crazy. It felt as if a thousand ants were crawling around on it.

"It's so gross!" Luke yelled behind me. "My face — it hurts!"

Down, down into the heavy darkness.

And then a flare of bright light made me shut my eyes.

Was it daylight? Were we heading outside?

No.

36

I forced my eyes open and squinted at the yellow light.

And realized I was staring at blazing flames.

The slide ahead of us was on fire!

The yellow-and-orange flames raged up, topped by a curtain of billowing black smoke.

I raised my hands to my face and started to shriek.

We were sliding right into the blazing flames.

"We're going to burn up!" Luke screamed. "Help — somebody! Help us!"

8

I shut my eyes and felt a powerful burst of heat, almost like an explosion.

I'm burning up! I thought.

Burning up!

A *whoosh* of cool air made me open my eyes.

The fire was behind us now. We had sailed right through it.

Curving gently, we slid through cool darkness. I could still see the orange flicker of flames reflected on the dark walls above us.

Luke and I were both silent. I was waiting for my heart to stop thudding in my chest.

"Great special effects!" Luke cried. He let out a wild laugh, a frantic laugh I'd never heard before.

The fire was fake, I realized. Some kind of projection or something.

I sucked in mouthfuls of the cool air. I had never been so terrified in my life.

"When does this ride end?" Luke cried. His voice had become high and frightened.

Never, I thought glumly. We really are going to slide forever.

And as that frightening thought lingered in my mind, a chute opened in front of us. Daylight streamed in.

Bump.

I landed hard on soft grass.

A few seconds later, Luke dropped out behind me.

I blinked several times, waiting for my eyes to adjust to the bright sunlight.

Then I climbed slowly to my feet, my heart still pounding.

A yellow-and-green sign on a wooden pole stood directly in front of us. It read: *WELCOME TO DOOM. POPULATION: 0 HUMANS.*

Standing next to the sign was Clay. He came rushing over to greet us, a happy smile on his round, pink face. "Hey, guys — hey!" he called. "Where've you been?" He slapped Luke a high five. Then Luke gave him a playful punch in the stomach.

"Where've *we* been?" I asked. "Where've *you* been?"

"Right here," Clay replied. "I didn't know where I was. I think this is the other side of the park or something. So I just waited for you."

"We went back on the Doom Slide," Luke explained. "We took your slide. Number ten. What a ride! It was so *cool!*"

A few seconds ago, Luke had been shrieking in real terror. Now here he was, pretending he loved it, telling Clay how cool it was.

"You picked the good slide!" Luke told Clay. "Wow. It was excellent!"

"I was kind of scared," Clay confessed. "I mean, the fire — "

"Great special effects!" my brother exclaimed. "This park is awesome!"

Luke was such a phony. There was no way he would ever admit that he had been worried about Clay. And no way he'd admit that the long slide to Doom had terrified him.

But I was glad to see his old enthusiasm return. I really didn't like seeing my brother frightened and in a panic.

"It *was* kind of a long slide," Clay said, frowning. His feathery blond hair glowed in the bright sunlight. "A little *too* long, I think."

"I'd like to go on it again!" Luke boasted.

I turned and gazed around. We were definitely in another section of HorrorLand. Nothing looked familiar.

Across the wide walkway, I saw several kids in bathing suits heading down a sandy path. A sign over the path read: *HORROR RAPIDS*.

To our right, a square-shaped building made of

glass reflected the bright sunlight. The glass walls shimmered brightly as if on fire. Squinting into the light, I could just barely make out the sign in front of it: *HOUSE OF MIRRORS*.

"Let's try the House of Mirrors!" Luke urged, pulling Clay by the arm.

"Whoa! Wait a minute!" I cried. "Don't you think we should try to find Mom and Dad?"

"They're way over on the other side of the park," Luke replied, tugging Clay along with him across the pavement. "Let's have some fun and *then* find them."

"They're probably looking for us," I said fretfully.

"The park isn't very crowded. They'll find us," Luke replied. "Come on, Lizzy — it looks like fun!"

I hesitated, thinking about Mom and Dad. I stared into the white glare of the glass building.

Suddenly, I felt someone tap my shoulder.

Startled, I cried out and spun around.

It was a green-costumed Horror. His bulging eyes stared into mine as he leaned close to me. *"Get away while you can!"* he whispered.

He turned his eyes quickly from side to side, as if making sure no one was watching him. *"Please — I'm serious! Get away while you can!"*

9

I was so stunned, I didn't say anything. I watched him run off, moving awkwardly in the bulky Horror costume, his purple tail dragging over the pavement behind him.

"What did he want?" Clay called. He and Luke were nearly up to the House of Mirrors entrance.

"He — he said we should get out while we can," I stammered, running over to them. I lost them for a moment in the blinding sunlight reflected off the glass building.

Luke laughed. "These Horror guys are great!" he declared. "They really try to scare you in this place!"

Behind his glasses, Clay's eyes narrowed thoughtfully. "He was kidding — right?" he asked quietly. "I mean, it was just a joke, wasn't it?"

"I don't know," I told him. "I guess so." I watched the Horror disappear quickly behind a tall, blue, pyramid-shaped building.

"That's his job," Luke insisted. "He goes around scaring people all day."

"Maybe he was really warning us," Clay murmured, staring at me.

"No way!" Luke declared. He gave Clay a hard slap on the back. "Stop looking so gloomy all the time. This is a great place! You *like* to be scared, don't you?"

Clay's expression remained worried. "I guess," he replied uncertainly.

I started to tell Clay I was sure it was just a joke, but Luke interrupted. "Hurry up! Let's check out the House of Mirrors. Let's have some fun before Mom and Dad show up and make us leave."

He dragged Clay toward the entrance, and I followed. We passed another *NO PINCHING* sign as we made our way to the shimmering glass building.

Outside the entrance, I stopped to read the yellow-and-green sign. It read: *HOUSE OF MIRRORS. REFLECT BEFORE YOU ENTER. NO ONE MAY EVER SEE YOU AGAIN!*

"Hey — wait up!" I called to the boys. They had already hurried inside.

I stepped in and found myself in a narrow, dark tunnel. My eyes were still filled with the bright glare from outside. I couldn't see a thing.

"Luke, Clay — wait up!" I shouted. My voice

echoed through the low tunnel. I could hear them laughing up ahead.

I jogged blindly, ducking my head because the ceiling was so low. Finally, my eyes adjusted to the darkness.

The tunnel ended, and I found myself in a narrow corridor with mirrored walls and a mirrored ceiling.

"Oh!" I uttered a low cry. I could see my reflections — dozens of them. I seemed to surround myself!

I stopped for a moment and adjusted my long, black braid. It was always coming loose. Then I called again to the boys, "Where are you? Wait up!"

I could hear them giggling somewhere up ahead. "Try and find us!" Luke called. More giggling.

I made my way quickly through the mirrored walkway. The walls curved to the right, then the left. My reflections followed me, stretching deep into the mirrors, dozens and dozens of me, getting smaller and smaller, stretching to infinity!

"Hey — don't get too far ahead!" I cried.

I heard them giggling. Then I heard a rumble of footsteps that seemed to come from the other side of the mirrored wall.

I followed the corridor, walking slowly, carefully, until I saw a narrow opening up ahead.

"Wait right there. I'm coming through!" I called.

I started through the opening, and — *BONK!* — hit my forehead on solid glass.

"Ow!" I cried out as the pain jolted across my forehead, then down the back of my neck, all the way down my spine.

I raised my hands to the glass and waited for my dizziness to fade away.

"Lizzy, where are you? Try to find us!" I heard Luke call.

"I hit my head!" I shouted, rubbing my forehead.

I could hear him and Clay laughing. Their voices seemed to be behind me now. I turned back, but there were only mirrors behind me. No opening.

My head still ached a little, but the dizziness had gone away. I started walking again, more carefully this time. I kept both hands out in front of me so I wouldn't bump into anything again.

I turned a corner and stepped into a different room. To my surprise, the floor in this room was a mirror. The walls, the ceiling, the floor — were all mirrors. I felt as if I were standing inside a mirrored box.

I took a few careful steps. It felt so weird walking on my own reflection.

I could see the tops and the bottoms of my sneakers as I walked. It made it really hard to walk. I kept having the feeling that I was going to fall into myself!

"Hey, guys — where are you?" I called.

No reply.

I felt a sharp stab of fear in my stomach.

"Luke? Clay? Are you there?" I saw the mouths of my reflections move as I called out, dozens of mouths. But only one voice came out, my voice, tiny and shrill.

"Luke? Clay?"

Silence.

"Don't fool around, guys!" I shouted. "Where are you?"

Silence. No reply.

I stared at the dozens of reflections on all sides of me. They all looked very frightened.

"Luke? Clay?"

Where had they gone?

10

I stared at my reflections as horrifying thoughts swept over me.

Had the boys really disappeared?

Had they fallen into some kind of trap? Were they lost in the maze of glass and mirrors?

HorrorLand was *too* scary, I decided. It was fun to be scared. But it was too hard to tell whether the scares here were for fun — or for real. Were there dangers in this place? Or was it all a big, scary joke?

"Luke? Clay?" I called to them in a trembling voice, turning all around, searching for an exit.

Silence.

Then I heard a muffled giggle.

Then I heard whispering voices. Nearby.

Another giggle, louder this time. Luke's giggle.

They had been playing a little joke on me. "Hey, you're not funny!" I screamed angrily. "Really! Not funny!"

I could hear them both burst out laughing.

"Come and find us, Lizzy!" Luke called.

"What's taking you so long?" Clay added.

More giggling. It seemed to come from just up ahead.

Sliding my hands along the mirrors, I followed the hallway around to the right. I had to duck my head to slip through a narrow opening between the mirrors.

I found myself in another small room surrounded by mirrors above and below and on all sides. The mirrors were tilted at strange angles so that my reflections appeared to bounce off each other as I moved.

"Where are you? Am I getting closer?" I called.

The light grew dim as I made my way through this room. My reflections darkened. The shadows grew longer.

"We can't see you!" Clay called.

"Hurry up!" Luke shouted impatiently.

"I'm going as fast as I can!" I screamed. "Just don't move, okay? Stay in one place."

"We are!" Luke called back.

"How will we ever get out of here?" I heard Clay ask him in a low voice.

"Ow!" I bumped my head again on a section of clear glass.

I pounded my fist angrily on the glass.

This wasn't any fun, I decided. It was too painful.

"Hurry up!" Luke called from somewhere nearby. "It's boring waiting here for you!"

"I'm coming," I muttered, rubbing my poor, aching forehead.

I turned a corner and stepped into a wider room. No mirrors here. The walls were all glass. I stopped to gaze around — and there was Luke.

"Finally!" he cried. "Why couldn't you find us?"

"I kept hitting my head," I told him. "Let's get out of here. Where's Clay?"

"Huh?" Luke's mouth dropped open in surprise. He spun around, searching for his friend. "He was standing right here," he said.

"Luke — I'm in no mood for any more dumb jokes," I said sharply. "Clay, where are you hiding?"

"I'm not hiding. I'm over here," Clay called.

I took a few steps closer to my brother, and Clay came into view. He was standing in deep shadows behind a glass wall, his hands pressed against the pane.

"How'd you get over there?" Luke asked Clay.

Clay shrugged. "I can't find a way out."

I moved toward my brother, then stopped. I suddenly realized that he was behind a wall of glass. Luke and I were in different rooms.

"Hey — where's the opening?" I asked him.

Luke glanced around. "What do you mean, Lizzy?"

"You and I — we're not in the same room," I replied. I walked up to the glass wall and tapped on it with my fist.

"Huh?" Luke's face filled with surprise. He made his way over to me. Then he tapped on his side of the glass, as if making sure it really did exist.

"How'd that get there?" he murmured.

Clay started moving around his room, sliding his hands along the panes of glass, searching for the opening.

"Stand right there," I told Luke. "I'll find a way into your room."

I followed Clay's example. I moved slowly around the room, keeping a hand pressed against the glass. The light was dim. My shadow fell over the glass as I walked. I could see my face reflected darkly in the glass. My eyes stared back at me, dark and desperate.

Before I realized it, I had made a complete circle.

I was back where I had started. And there was no opening. No doorway.

No way out.

"Hey! I'm trapped in here!" Clay called shrilly.

"So am I," I told him.

"There's *got* to be an opening," Luke said. "How did we get in?"

"You're right," I replied fretfully. "We should

be able to get out the way we came in." I began to search along the walls again, moving quickly.

My heart began to pound. I had a fluttering feeling in my chest. There *had* to be a way out. There *had* to be.

Luke pounded hard on the glass. In the other room, I could see Clay jogging frantically around his room, pushing on the walls as he moved.

I went all the way around twice, then stopped. There was no way out.

"I — I'm trapped," I stammered. "It's like a box. A glass box."

"We're *all* trapped!" Clay cried.

Luke was still pounding frantically on the glass with his fists. "Luke — stop!" I cried shrilly. "That isn't helping!"

He lowered his fists to his sides. "This is ridiculous," he muttered. "There's got to be a way out."

"Maybe there's a trapdoor or something," I suggested. I began to search the mirrored floor. It was too dark to see well. The floor appeared solid to me.

I returned to the glass wall. "This isn't much fun," I said glumly.

Luke and Clay nodded. I could see they were both really frightened. So was I. But I decided I was two years older than them, so I had to try to be the brave one.

I wasn't feeling very brave, though. Uttering a worried sigh, I leaned against the wall that separated Luke and me.

And as I leaned, the wall started to move.

I jumped back with a sharp cry.

The wall was sliding toward me, closing in on me.

I took another step back.

Glancing around frantically, I saw that *all* the walls were sliding in.

"Luke!" I cried. I turned to see him backing up, too.

"The walls!" Clay called. "Help me!"

"They're sliding in on me, too!" Luke screamed. "Each room must have its own glass walls!"

All three of us were trapped.

With a desperate groan, I threw myself against one of the walls and tried to push it back.

But I couldn't stop it.

The box was closing in, growing smaller. Smaller.

"We're going to be crushed!" I cried.

11

"Do something! Please — do something!" Clay was screaming.

Luke lowered his shoulder to the glass and struggled to stop it from moving. But he wasn't strong enough. The walls kept sliding in on him.

I backed up, my hands raised like a shield.

Closer, closer. The glass walls moved slowly, silently.

I backed up until my back hit the wall behind me.

There was nowhere to go.

"Do something! Somebody — *do something!*" Clay's terrified screams rang in my ears.

"The glass — it's *squeezing* me!" Luke shrieked. "Lizzy — !"

"I — I can't move!" I shouted to him.

The panes of glass began to press in on me from all sides. Above and below, too.

I suddenly pictured one of those crushed cars. You know. The cars that are crunched into a perfect square in those big compactor machines.

My entire body shuddered as I realized I was going to be crushed into a perfect square, too.

"Ow!" I cried out as the glass pressed down on me. "Somebody — help!" I tried to scream, but my voice came out a muffled yelp.

It was getting hard to breathe.

The glass panes moved in. Tighter. Tighter.

I gasped for air.

I tried to push with all my might against the glass.

But it was no use.

I was being crushed into a human square.

12

I couldn't hear Luke or Clay anymore.

I could only hear my gasping, choked breaths.

I shut my eyes.

And felt the floor drop away.

And before I realized what was happening, I was falling, falling rapidly down.

I opened my eyes in time to see the glass walls roll above me as I slid down, down, down through an open chute.

And in a few seconds, I was back outside. I landed sitting up on the grass with a gentle *thud*.

Luke and Clay came sliding out beside me.

For a long moment, we sat on the grass, blinking in the bright sunlight, staring at each other in disbelief.

"We're okay," Clay said uncertainly, finally breaking the silence. He slowly climbed to his feet. His round face was bright red, and his glasses were crooked and nearly falling off his nose. "We're okay!"

Luke let out a laugh. A gleeful laugh. He stood up and began jumping up and down for joy.

I didn't exactly feel like jumping up and down. I was still picturing the crushed car.

Luke reached down, grabbed both of my hands, and pulled me to my feet. "What should we do next?" he demanded, grinning.

"Huh? Next?" I cried. "Are you for real?"

"That was really scary," Clay said, his face still red. "I thought we were going to be scrunched flat."

"It was awesome!" Luke declared.

Once again, he was forgetting that a few seconds before, he'd been screaming in total panic.

"It was way too scary," Clay murmured, shaking his head.

"Clay's right," I agreed. "It was too scary to be fun. One more second, and . . ."

"Don't you see? That's the whole idea!" Luke cried. "That's how they scare you here. It's so awesome! They make you think that one more second and you're a goner. But it's all perfectly timed. They want you to be terrified — and, then — *poof* — you're okay!"

"I guess you're right," said Clay doubtfully. He pushed up his glasses, then rubbed his chin.

"We're not really going to get hurt or anything," Luke continued. "This is an amusement park, remember? They want you to come back again and again. So they're not going to really hurt any-body."

"Maybe," Clay said.

"But, Luke, what if they mess up?" I asked him. "What if the machines get goofed up? What if the timing gets off? Let's say the floor underneath us got stuck. Then what?"

Luke didn't reply. He stared back at me thoughtfully.

"What would have happened to us if the floor hadn't dropped away at the right moment?" I demanded.

Luke shrugged. "They make sure everything works okay," he answered finally.

I rolled my eyes. "Yeah. Sure."

"Is it possible to really be scared to *death*?" Clay asked me, a solemn expression on his face. "I mean, I know it happens in books and movies. But does it happen in real life?"

"I don't know. Maybe," I replied.

"I'll bet people could get scared to death in that House of Mirrors," Clay continued seriously.

"No way!" Luke insisted. "Listen to me. This is just a place for fun. Scary fun."

He was watching something over my shoulder. I turned to see one of the guys in a green Horror costume walking by, carrying a huge bouquet of black balloons.

Luke hurried up beside the Horror. "Hey, has

anyone ever died here in this park?" Luke asked.

The Horror kept walking. The black balloons bobbed above his head. "Only once," he told Luke.

"One person died here?" Luke asked.

The Horror shook his big green head. "No. Not what I meant."

"What did you mean?" Luke demanded.

"A person can only die once here," the Horror said. "No one has ever died twice."

13

"Do you mean people have *really died* here?" I shouted.

But the Horror walked quickly on, the black balloons bouncing against each other, floating darkly against the clear blue sky.

The Horror's answer made me shiver. It wasn't just his words. It was the cold tone of his voice, the way he made it sound like a warning.

"He was joking — right?" Clay asked in a trembling voice. He scratched his blond hair nervously.

"Yeah. I guess," I replied.

A family walked past us, heading toward the House of Mirrors. They had two little boys with them, both about five or six, and both of them were crying.

"I've seen so many crying kids in this park!" I commented.

"They're just wimps," Luke replied. "Scaredy-cats. Let's go find another ride or something."

"No. I really think we should find Mom and Dad," I told him.

"Yeah. Let's go find them," Clay said eagerly. The poor kid. I think he was really scared. But he was trying his best not to let my brother see how frightened he was.

"Aw, what's the hurry?" Luke protested. "Let them find *us*."

"But they're probably really worried," I insisted. I started walking toward the front gate.

"Dad will only make us leave," Luke grumbled. But he followed anyway. And Clay gratefully came along, keeping close to my side.

Following the trail, we passed by a rickety, old wooden roller coaster. It rose up as high as a four-story building, casting a wide, dark shadow over the walk. A sign in front read: *OUT OF ORDER. DO YOU DARE TO RIDE IT ANYWAY?*

The gate was open. There was no attendant.

"Hey, Lizzy, want to ride it?" Luke asked, staring at the beat-up old cars parked at the bottom of the tracks.

"No way!" Clay and I replied in unison. We kept on walking.

The trail curved under thick trees, and we were suddenly in the shade. A sign read: *BEWARE OF TREE SNAKES*.

Clay covered his head with his hands. All three of us raised our eyes to the trees.

Were there really snakes up there?

It was too dark to see anything. The leaves were so thick, no sunlight filtered through.

Suddenly, I heard a gentle hissing sound.

At first I thought it was just the rustle of the leaves.

But then the hissing grew louder — until all of the trees seemed to be hissing down at us.

"Run!" I cried.

The three of us started running along the trail, ducking low, our sneakers thudding hard on the pavement. The hissing in the trees above us grew louder, angrier.

I thought I saw a long, dark snake slithering in the grass beside the trail. But it might have just been a shadow.

We kept running even after the trees ended and we were in sunlight again. The trail curved past a row of evil-looking statues. They were made of stone. They were statues of grinning monsters, eyes narrowed menacingly, fangs lowered from their twisted mouths. Their arms were out-stretched, ready to grab anyone who came close.

I slowed to a trot, my eyes on the ugly statues. Suddenly I heard low, evil laughter.

"It — it's coming from the statues!" Clay exclaimed. "Keep running!"

Did the statues move toward us? Did they raise their arms higher? Did they beckon to us to come closer?

I'm not sure. With their evil laughter in my

ears, I lowered my head and turned on the speed.

All three of us were panting hard as we ran along the trail. I didn't see any other people. I didn't see anyone in a Horror costume, either.

We slowed as we came to another sign. This one had an arrow pointing in the direction we were running. It read: *FRONT EXIT. DON'T BOTHER. YOU WILL NEVER ESCAPE.*

I caught the worried expression on Clay's face as he read the sign. "It's only a joke," I told him. "The signs are supposed to be funny."

"Ha-ha," he said weakly. He was panting hard, struggling to catch his breath.

Without warning, Luke jumped on Clay's shoulders. "Hey, Clay — how about a ride?"

Clay cried out angrily, "Get off!"

Luke laughed and hung on. Clay dropped to his knees, trying to throw Luke off.

"Come on, guys," I pleaded. "Luke, stop being such a goof. We're trying to find Mom and Dad."

But now they were laughing and wrestling on the ground.

"Come *on*, guys!" I shouted, rolling my eyes. "Let's go!" I tugged my brother to his feet.

Clay's glasses had flown off. He stopped to pick them up from the grass. Then we continued on our way.

The path led past a rectangular flower garden — filled with black flowers! Then it suddenly came to a stop in front of a large, red barn.

The boys walked up to the open doorway of the barn. I stayed back, searching for a path that led around the barn. I couldn't see one.

"The path goes right through the barn to the other side," Luke called to me. "Come on, Lizzy!" He motioned for me to join them.

I spotted a small sign painted to the right of the barn's double doors. It read: *BAT BARN*.

"Hey — are there bats in there?" I called, feeling a cold shudder run down my back. I like most animals. But bats really give me the creeps.

Luke stepped inside the barn. Clay hung back, standing just outside the door. "I don't see any," Luke called out to me. "It's kind of dark."

A strange odor invaded my nostrils. It was strong and sour. It came from the barn.

I didn't want to go in there.

"Come on, Lizzy!" Luke called. "The path goes right out the other side. Don't be chicken. You can run straight through."

I stepped up beside Clay at the doorway and peered inside the barn.

"It looks okay," Clay said quietly.

The sour odor was much stronger. "Yuck," I said, making a face. "It really stinks."

Luke stood inside the barn, his eyes raised to the rafters. "I don't see anything up there," he reported.

Doors on the opposite wall were wide open. It would only take ten seconds to run through the barn and out the other side, I realized.

"Let's go," I told Clay.

He and I stepped into the barn. The sour smell was overpowering. I held my breath and pinched my fingers over my nose.

We started running to the doors on the opposite wall — and they slammed shut.

With a gasp of surprise, I turned back to the doors we had entered. They slammed shut, too.

"Hey — !" I shouted angrily.

"What's going on?" Clay cried in a whisper.

We were in total darkness, blacker than black.

The sour odor swept over me. I started to feel sick.

And then I heard the rapid flutter of wings. Soft at first, then louder, closer.

I screamed as I felt something brush against the back of my neck.

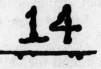

14

"Go away!" I let out a low moan of horror and swung my hands wildly above my head.

The rapid fluttering retreated, then returned.

"Bats!" Clay cried in a terrified, tiny voice. I felt him grab my arm.

"I can't see!" Luke shouted. "It's so dark!"

"I — I hate bats!" I stammered.

I felt a cold *whoosh* of air as a bat flapped over my head.

I swung my hands wildly.

The flapping, fluttering sounds were all around us.

As my eyes slowly adjusted to the darkness, I began to see shadowy shapes shooting past. Back and forth. Faster and faster.

I felt one brush my shoulder.

"Oh, help!" I cried.

Clay started to shriek. "Help us! Help us!"

"They're zooming right at me!" Luke wailed.

Something bumped into my shoulder. I screamed.

"Help us! Help us!" Clay continued to plead at the top of his lungs. His shouts were nearly drowned out by the flapping of wings.

I felt another bat brush against my shoulder. Covering my face, I tried to make my way blindly to the door.

The sour odor choked me. My terror made my legs shaky. I could barely walk.

And then I felt a hard tug in my hair.

Another tug. Loud flapping right on my head.

A shrill whistling hiss. So close, it could have been coming from *me*.

I screamed. I screamed again.

"It — it's caught in my hair!" I cried, falling to my knees.

Another shrill hiss. Another tug of my hair.

I swung my hands. I hit it. I felt a warm body, felt the brush of fluttering wings.

I shoved it hard — shoved it from my hair.

"Ohhh, help!" I cried.

The flapping wings and shrill whistles surrounded me. I could hear Luke and Clay shouting. But they seemed far, far away.

Another one brushed my cheek. Another one bumped my shoulder.

The shadows darted back and forth. The barn was alive with flying, chittering bats.

"Ohh, help! Help us, please!"

Another one brushed my face. I felt a rush of air, beating wings on the top of my head.

"Help us! Help us!"

But there was no one around to help.

15

I covered my eyes with one hand and thrashed out wildly with the other hand, trying to beat the bats away.

Choking and sobbing, I could barely breathe.

I heard Luke calling, far, far away. He seemed to be behind a curtain of flapping, chittering bats.

And then, suddenly, sunlight invaded the barn.

On my knees, I lowered my hand from my eyes and saw that the barn door had slid open.

Luke, standing at the door, his mouth open in shock, turned back to Clay and me. "I — I touched the door, and it opened," he explained.

Clay's glasses were hanging off one ear. His blond hair was totally messed up. His eyes darted around the barn. "Where are the bats?" he cried.

I raised my eyes to the rafters. "Hey — !" I cried out. No bats. No sign of any bats anywhere.

I climbed to my feet, pulling my hair back with both hands. "Let's get out of here!" I cried.

Clay and I followed Luke out of the barn. The warm sunshine felt so good!

I was still itchy from the bats. I rubbed my shoulders and the back of my neck. "I *hate* bats! I really do!" I exclaimed with a shudder.

"But there weren't any bats," Luke said, grinning at me. "It was all a fake."

"Huh? It was not!" Clay cried angrily. "Those were bats. I could hear them — and feel them!"

"All special effects," Luke claimed.

"It wasn't special effects when one got tangled in my hair!" I cried. Just thinking about it gave me cold shivers.

"Special effects," Luke repeated. "Really excellent special effects. I was almost scared, too."

"Almost?" I cried. I walked over, grabbed him, and pretended to wring his neck. "Almost? I heard you screaming your head off, Luke!"

He pulled out of my grasp, laughing. "I knew it wasn't real. I was just screaming like that to scare you!"

What a liar! I really didn't believe my brother. He was scared. He was plenty scared. I *knew* he was!

"They were bats, not special effects," I insisted angrily.

"Then where did they go when the door opened?" Luke demanded. "As soon as the door opened, the bats all vanished."

"Let's stop talking about it," Clay pleaded. "Let's find your parents — okay?"

"Yeah, okay," I agreed, glaring at Luke. "You really are nuts, you know that?" I told him.

He stuck his tongue out at me.

I wanted to punch his lights out. But I try to be a nonviolent person. So I just gave him one hard punch on the shoulder.

He howled in protest. "You're stupid, Lizzy. You're really stupid," he muttered. "And you're afraid of *pretend* bats!"

I ignored him and led the way down the path toward the front gate. Two people in Horror costumes appeared on the path, going the other way, chatting enthusiastically.

"Is this the way to the front gate?" I called to them.

They ignored my question and walked right past us.

"Hey — !" I called to them.

But they both kept jabbering away and didn't even seem to see or hear me.

The sun beamed down on us. The air had become hot and still, with no breeze at all.

I wiped sweat off my forehead with one hand. I could still smell the sour aroma of the Bat Barn. The odor was on my hands, on my clothes.

I saw four teenagers in bathing suits, two boys and two girls, hurrying over the grass toward a large, brown pond. A sign came into view near the shore. It read: *ALLIGATOR POND. FEEL FREE TO SWIM HERE.*

Luke laughed. "Are those guys crazy?"

We stopped to watch them step into the water.

"Do you think there are really alligators in there?" Clay asked, biting his lower lip.

I shrugged. "Who knows? I don't know *what* to think about this park!"

We continued along the path. A few minutes later, I recognized the mountain-shaped structure of the Doom Slide. The wide, circular plaza came into view. It was nearly deserted. Even the ice-cream-selling Horror had vanished from his cart.

"Where do you suppose Mom and Dad are?" I asked.

"They've probably been looking for us for hours, and now they're really mad," Luke said, frowning.

"Where *are* they?" Clay cried. He was starting to sound really stressed out. "We've *got* to find them."

"Is that them?" Luke asked. He was pointing to a man and a woman in the shade of a large stone fountain.

I shielded my eyes from the sun with one hand. The woman was tall, with dark hair. The man was short and blond.

"Yes! That's them!" I cried happily. I started running to the fountain, calling to them, "Mom! Dad!"

The boys came racing after me.

"Mom! Dad! Hey — !" I shouted happily.

They both turned around, surprised expressions on their faces.

"Oh!" I cried out when I saw it wasn't them. I stopped short, and Luke bumped right into me.

"Sorry," I told the confused couple. "We thought you were someone else."

The three of us hurried across the plaza. I could hear the wail of wolf howls from the Werewolf Village. The ice-cream cart stood lonely and deserted near the entrance to the Doom Slide.

"Where *are* they?" Clay asked, whining. "I'm starting to get hungry."

"Yeah. It's way past lunchtime," I agreed.

"They could be anywhere," Luke said unhappily, kicking a pebble across the pavement. "They could be anywhere in this giant park."

I sighed. "Let's look for them in the shade. The sun is really getting hot."

We headed toward the shade of the Doom Slide building. Suddenly, two green-costumed Horrors came into view. Their big, yellow eyes bulged in front of their heads.

Without thinking, I went running up to them. "Have you seen our parents?" I asked breathlessly.

They stared at me in surprise. "Your parents?" one of them repeated.

"Yeah." I nodded. "My mom has black hair. My dad is kind of short and he has blond hair."

"Hmmmm." The two Horrors glanced at each other.

"Mom was wearing a bright yellow sundress," I told them.

"And Dad had a Chicago Cubs cap on his head," Luke added.

"Oh, yeah. Right," one of the Horrors, a woman, replied.

"You saw them?" I asked eagerly.

She nodded. "Yeah. I remember them. They left. They left about half an hour ago."

"Huh?" I gaped at her in disbelief.

"They asked me to give you a message," the Horror said.

"Message? What message?" I asked.

"Good-bye," the Horror replied.

16

"You're wrong!" I cried. "They wouldn't leave."

"About half an hour ago," the Horror repeated. She shrugged her shoulders under the bulky monster costume. "I was at the gate when they left."

"But — but — " I sputtered.

The two Horrors turned and began walking toward a small white shed at the edge of the plaza.

"Hey, wait!" I called, chasing after them. "You made a mistake. Our parents wouldn't leave without us."

They disappeared into the shed. The door slammed behind them.

I turned back to Luke and Clay. They stared at me blankly.

"She was wrong," I told them. "Mom and Dad are still here. I know it."

"Then why did she say — " Clay started, but his voice broke. I could see that he was very worried and upset. Beads of sweat ran down his pink forehead.

Luke tried to make a joke. "I guess that means we have the whole park to ourselves!" he exclaimed, forcing a smile.

"Very funny," I replied sarcastically. "We also have no money, and we're about three hundred miles from home."

"We could call somebody," Luke suggested.

"No phones," Clay muttered. He lowered his head, shoved his hands into the pockets of his shorts, and turned away from us.

"Oh, right," Luke remembered. "They told Dad there are no phones in the park."

"That's crazy," I said heatedly. "They're liars. The Horrors are all liars."

"I guess that's their job," Luke said. "Telling us lies to scare us to death. That's why they call it HorrorLand."

"They should call it DumbLand," Clay muttered bitterly.

"But it's so cool!" Luke protested. "I *love* being scared out of my wits. Don't you?" He gave Clay a hard shove.

"No," Clay replied softly. He made no attempt to shove Luke back.

"Well, she was lying about Mom and Dad," I insisted, gazing at the white shed. "She was just trying to scare us. Mom and Dad are still here. We just have to find them."

"Come on, let's go," Luke urged. "I hope we find them soon. I'm getting really hungry."

We wandered through the park for what seemed like hours. We searched through dark, mysterious woods and strange monster villages. We passed through a carnival area with dozens of scary-looking rides.

On the other side of a Vampire Village, we passed a building marked Monster Zoo. It was closed. But we could hear the most terrifying grunts, howls, and moans coming from inside.

A long yellow building had a sign outside that proclaimed: *GUILLOTINE MUSEUM. PLEASE HOLD ON TO YOUR HEAD.* Luke wanted to go inside, but Clay and I talked him out of it.

HorrorLand was surprisingly empty. We passed several Horrors scurrying along the paths in their bright green costumes. And we saw a few families wandering around, always with crying kids.

The rides in the carnival area were all running empty. All of the food stands and restaurants were empty, too.

We walked clear across to the other end of the park. I was feeling more and more worried.

Why hadn't we run into Mom and Dad?

Surely we should have seen them by now.

Clay had become very quiet. I could tell he was really scared. Even Luke trudged along with his shoulders slumped and his head down.

By the time we found ourselves back at the

Alligator Pond, I was feeling pretty bad. I crossed the grassy shore and walked up to the edge of the brown water.

"What do you think happened to those teen-agers who went swimming here?" Luke asked, staring across the pond. "Think the alligators ate them?"

"Maybe," I replied. I wasn't really listening to him. I was thinking about Mom and Dad.

"Hey, look!" Clay cried, pointing to the water.

I saw two long, greenish-brown logs floating toward us on top of the water. It took me a while to realize that the logs were alligators.

"Big ones!" Clay declared in a hushed whisper.

"Better step back," I warned them.

All three of us were standing on the water's edge. The alligators floated silently just below the surface of the still water, hardly creating a ripple.

"Mom and Dad didn't leave without us," I repeated for the thousandth time.

"But we searched everywhere," Luke said quietly.

"They didn't leave without us," I said. "They would never leave without us. So . . ." I hesitated. I was thinking hard, and my thoughts were all frightening.

"So?" Clay asked eagerly.

"So if they're not in the park," I continued, "it means something happened to them. Something bad happened to them."

Clay gasped. Luke narrowed his blue eyes at me. "What do you mean, Lizzy?" he asked.

"I mean maybe this place really is evil," I said. "And maybe the Horrors or somebody did something bad to Mom and Dad."

I stared down at the brown alligator backs gliding so smoothly, so effortlessly toward us.

"That's crazy," Luke muttered.

I knew it was crazy. But I had no other explanation.

"I have such a bad feeling about this park," I told them. "A real bad feeling."

And as I said that, I felt strong hands grab me from behind and push me into the Alligator Pond.

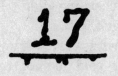

17

I screamed.

Then I realized I wasn't being tossed into the water.

The hands were holding on to my shoulders.

I spun around. "Dad!" I cried.

"Lizzy!" he exclaimed, still holding on to me. "Where have you guys been?"

"We've searched this entire park twelve times!" Mom declared. She was standing behind us on the grass, hands pressed tensely on her waist.

"We were looking for *you!*" I cried.

"They told us you left!" Luke said.

"We were kind of scared," Clay added.

We all started talking at once. I was so happy to see them. And I could see that Luke and Clay were really happy, too.

I had imagined all sorts of terrible things happening to Mom and Dad. It wasn't like me to let my imagination run away like that.

But HorrorLand was such a scary place. It was

impossible not to have scary thoughts here.

"I want to go home," I said.

"Did you find a phone?" Clay asked. "Did you find a car?"

Dad shook his head. "No. No phones. The guy in the monster costume didn't lie. There are no phones in the park."

"But the Horrors were very nice to us," Mom broke in. "They told us not to worry about a thing."

"They said to just come to the ticket booth when we were ready to leave," Dad reported.

Mom ran a hand tenderly through Luke's hair. "Did you go on any rides or anything?"

"We did a lot of scary stuff," Luke told her.

"Very scary," Clay added.

"I'm really hungry," Luke said.

Dad glanced at his watch. "It's way past lunchtime. I think we're all hungry."

"The restaurants and foodstands are all on the other side of the park," Mom said.

"Can we just eat lunch and then leave?" I asked eagerly. I still had a bad feeling about the place. I wanted to get away from HorrorLand, far away.

"Your mom and I have spent all our time searching for you," Dad said, wiping sweat off his sunburnt forehead with one hand. "We haven't had any fun at all."

"We should all at least go on one ride together before we leave," Mom said.

"I just want to go," I urged. "I really do."

"Lizzy, that's not like you," Mom scolded.

"She's scared," Luke told them. "She's a chicken."

"Maybe there's a ride that will take us to the front of the park," Dad suggested. "We could all take it, then have some lunch and leave."

"That sounds good," Mom said. She stared at me. "Okay with you?"

"I guess," I told her, sighing. "It's just that the rides here are all too scary. They aren't any fun."

Luke laughed. "They're too scary for Lizzy — but not for Clay and me," he said. "Right, Clay?"

"I was a *little* scared in the Bat Barn," Clay confessed.

We headed away from the Alligator Pond, across the grassy shore to the paved walkway. A couple of costumed Horrors walked past, chattering in low voices.

A girl's high-pitched shrieks of terror floated in the air from somewhere in the distance. The same frightening cry repeated over and over.

Wolf howls rose up in front of us. And from a speaker hidden somewhere in the trees, I heard evil laughter, a hideous cackle that repeated over and over.

"It's like being in a horror movie," Mom commented.

"Very clever," Dad added, walking with a hand

on my shoulder. "It's strange that we never heard of this park."

"They should put some ads on TV," Mom said. "Then they'd get more people to come here."

We passed by a tall, narrow, green building with a sign in front that read: *FREE FALL. THE ONLY BUNGEE JUMP WITHOUT A CORD.*

"Want to try that?" Dad asked, squeezing my shoulder and grinning at me.

"I don't think so," I quickly replied.

Luke was way ahead of us. He turned around and walked backwards, waiting for us to catch up. "Mom and Dad should try the Doom Slide," he said, grinning. "It's awesome!"

Had he really forgotten how terrified he was?

"I don't think they'd like it," I said quietly.

"Maybe we could find something that's just a *little* scary," Clay suggested.

Dad laughed. "Are you having a good time, Clay?"

Clay hesitated. "A little," he replied finally.

"I'm having a *great* time!" Luke declared.

The path curved along a narrow, brown river. Millions of tiny white insects flitted over the surface of the water. Catching the bright sunlight, they looked like little, sparkling diamonds.

A small, brown boathouse came into view. Behind it, I could see slender canoes bobbing beneath a wooden dock.

A sign beside the boathouse read: *COFFIN CRUISE. A RELAXING FLOAT TO THE GRAVE.*

"This might be fun," Mom said, her eyes on the small boats.

"I think the river flows toward the front of the park," Dad said. "Let's take it!"

Luke cheered and went running to the dock.

I lingered behind the others. When I finally stepped out onto the dock, it took me a while to realize that the objects bobbing in the brown water weren't canoes — they were coffins!

They were made of black, polished wood. The lids were pulled back, revealing red satin interiors. Each coffin was big enough for one person.

I felt a cold chill run down my back. "We're really going to climb into coffins?" I asked.

"They look comfy," Mom said, smiling at me. "The water is flat and gentle, Lizzy. It won't be a scary ride."

"Me first!" Luke cried, running to the end of the wooden dock.

Two costumed Horrors appeared to help us into the coffins. "Lie back. Enjoy the ride," one of them said.

"It will be your last," the other Horror added with a low chuckle.

When we were all inside coffins, the Horrors untied them and gave us a hard push away from the dock.

Here I am, I thought, lying in my coffin.

Here we all are, my entire family, on our backs in our coffins.

The coffin floated gently, bobbing in the water. I stared up at the bright blue sky. Trees shimmered on both banks as I floated past.

It was so pretty, so relaxing.

Why did I think something terrible was about to happen?

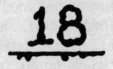

Lying on my back, I couldn't see the others over the coffin sides. But I could hear the splash of their coffins around mine.

"This is nice," Mom said. "Very relaxing."

"It's boring!" Luke declared from up ahead of me. "Where's the scary part?"

"It's just a nice ride in a coffin," Dad said. "Do you think we're really floating? Or do you think the coffin is on some kind of track?"

"I could float like this for hours," Mom said.

"The rides here are pretty long," Clay told her.

"Is that a hawk up in the sky?" Dad asked. "Can everyone see it?"

Shielding my eyes from the sun with one hand, I searched the sky. Directly above, a dark shadow hovered high in the sky, a little bigger than a dot.

"It's not a hawk. I'll bet it's a vulture!" Luke declared. "It sees the coffins, and it's waiting to eat our flesh!" He laughed.

"Luke — where do you get these hideous ideas?" Mom demanded.

"Maybe Luke should *live* in HorrorLand!" Dad exclaimed. "We could get him one of those green monster costumes, and he'd fit right in perfectly!"

"He doesn't *need* a costume!" I joked. I was starting to feel a little better. The ride was gentle and relaxing. And I figured nothing terrible could happen with my whole family around.

I settled back on the coffin bottom, my hands resting at my sides, and stared up dreamily at the bird circling high in the clear sky. The coffin bobbed gently, making soft splashing sounds.

So pleasant . . .

So quiet . . .

And then, before I could utter a sound, the coffin lid slammed shut over me. And I was trapped in total darkness.

19

"Hey — !" I shouted. My voice was muffled by the heavy lid over me.

I could heard the dull *thud* of the other coffin lids slamming shut.

"Hey — let me out!"

I pushed against the lid with both hands. But it wouldn't budge.

I took a deep breath and tried again. This time, I pushed with my hands and my feet. The heavy lid still didn't move.

My heart was pounding so hard, I thought my chest would explode. The air inside the closed coffin was already getting hot and stuffy.

"Open up! Open up!" I screamed.

I tried pushing the lid again. I could hear Clay's muffled cries in the coffin next to mine. The poor guy was screaming his head off.

I let out a loud groan as I pushed up with all my strength. The lid wouldn't give an inch.

Calm down, Lizzy. Calm down, I instructed

myself. *It's just a stupid ride. The coffin lid will open any second.*

Breathing hard, I waited.

I counted to ten.

I counted to ten again.

The lid didn't snap open.

I tried shutting my eyes and counting to fifty. When I reach fifty, I told myself, I'll open my eyes, and the lid will be open.

" . . . twenty-two, twenty-three, twenty-four . . ." I counted out loud. My voice sounded tiny and choked. It was getting hard to breathe. The air began to feel really stale.

I stopped counting at twenty-five and opened my eyes. The lid hadn't popped open.

It's so hot in here, I thought. The sun is beating down on the lid. There's no air, and I'm going to fry!

I tried to scream, but no sound came out.

I gasped for air.

Outside, I could hear muffled shouts and cries.

Was that my *mother* screaming like that?

"It's just a ride," I said out loud. "Just a stupid ride. The lid is going to pop — *now!*"

But it didn't.

The air was so hot, so hot and stale.

Why didn't the lid open?

Why?

I tried to force back my panic, but I couldn't. My entire body was shaking and shivering. I felt cold perspiration drip down my forehead.

"Something has gone wrong!" I cried out loud. "The lid is supposed to open — but it doesn't!"

Frantically, I pushed up with both hands. My arms ached from pushing so hard. But the lid didn't move.

The coffin bobbed and rocked in the water.

I lowered my hands in defeat. I sucked in a mouthful of the hot, stale air. My chest was heaving. My body trembled.

And then I felt my legs start to itch. A tingly feeling down near my ankles.

Moving up my legs.

An itchy, crawly feeling.

Something was crawling slowly up my legs.

Something small and prickly.

"Ohh." I let out a low, terrified groan.

Spiders!

20

I tried to scratch my legs, but my arms weren't long enough. Unable to move or bend in the cramped coffin, I couldn't reach down to them.

The tingling moved higher.

I wanted to scream, but I started to cough.

And then the coffin lid popped open. Bright sunlight made me shut my eyes.

"Oh!" I pulled myself up to a sitting position. Blinking against the light, I saw the others already scrambling up out of their coffins.

I scratched my legs furiously. To my surprise, there were no spiders. No bugs of any kind.

The coffin had pulled up to a small dock. I braced both hands against the sides of the coffin and heaved myself to my feet.

"Let's get *out* of here!" I heard Clay cry.

"That was *horrible!*" my mom shrieked.

Luke didn't say anything. His face was pale, and his black hair was matted to his forehead with sweat.

"They really went too far!" Dad said angrily. "I'm going to complain."

"Let's just go!" Mom told him.

We all scrambled onto the dock. I helped pull Clay up. Then I took several deep breaths of fresh air.

Dad ran off the dock toward the open plaza, and the rest of us hurried after him. "To the ticket booth!" he called back to us. "Right up there!" He pointed.

The coffin ride had taken us to the front of the park. I could see the front gate and the row of green ticket booths to the right.

"That ride was really gross!" Clay said, shaking his head.

"My legs got all itchy. I thought it was ants!" Luke declared.

"I thought it was spiders!" I told him.

"I wonder how they *did* that," Luke said thoughtfully.

"I don't care," I replied. "I just want to get out of here. I hate this place!"

"So do I," Clay agreed.

"They just go too far," Mom said breathlessly, jogging to keep up with us as we followed Dad. "It isn't any fun when a ride is that scary. I really had trouble breathing."

"So did I," I told her.

"Hey, how do we get home?" Luke suddenly demanded, staring at Mom. "Our car blew up."

"I think those people in the monster costumes will lend us a car," Mom replied. "They told your father just to come to the ticket booth."

"Can we stop and get pizza?" Luke asked.

"Let's get out of this place and *then* worry about lunch," Mom told him.

The main plaza was totally empty. Not another living person.

We followed Dad to the first ticket booth. He turned back to us, making a disappointed face. "Closed," he said. A metal grate had been pulled over the window.

Dad was breathing hard from running all the way. He pushed his blond hair off his sweaty forehead with both hands. "Over here," he said.

We followed him to the next ticket booth. Also closed.

Then the next. Closed.

It didn't take us long to discover that *all* of the ticket booths were closed.

"Weird," Luke said, shaking his head.

"Don't they expect any more visitors today?" Mom asked Dad. "How can they just close up like that?"

Dad shrugged. "We'll have to ask someone." His eyes searched the empty grounds.

I turned and checked out the plaza along with him. Still no one in sight. No visitors. No Horrors.

"Let's try over there," Dad said. He started walking to a low, green building that stood beyond the ticket booths. It looked like some kind of office.

It was closed, too. Dad tried the door. It was locked.

Dad scratched his head. "What's going on here? Where'd everyone disappear to?" he demanded.

Mom took his arm. "It's very strange," she said softly.

I glanced at Luke and Clay. They were standing tensely side by side on the walk in front of the office. Neither of them spoke.

"Are you sure these are the right ticket booths?" I asked.

"Yes," Dad replied wearily. "This is the front entrance."

"So where can everyone be?" Mom asked, chewing her lower lip.

"Maybe we can find someone in the parking lot," I suggested. "You know. A parking attendant or something. They'll be able to tell us how to get a car to go home."

"Good idea, Lizzy," Dad said. He patted the top of my head, the way he used to when I was a little girl.

I waited for Luke to make fun of me. But he didn't say a word. I guess he was too worried and upset.

"Come on," I urged. I turned and ran past the empty ticket booths. The tall, metal front gate to HorrorLand stood just beyond the booths.

I stopped for a second to read a sign on the side

of one of the ticket booths. It said: *NO EXIT. NO ONE LEAVES HORRORLAND ALIVE!*

"Ha-ha," I said sarcastically. "These signs are a riot, aren't they?"

I jogged the rest of the way and reached the gate first. I pulled it, and it wouldn't open. So I tried pushing it.

It didn't move.

Then I saw the heavy chain and the large steel padlock on the gate.

Swallowing hard, I turned back to the others.

"We're locked in!" I told them.

21

"What?" Dad stared at me, his face twisted in confusion. I don't think he believed me.

"We're locked in!" I repeated. I lifted the heavy metal padlock with both hands and then let it fall back with a loud *clang* against the bars of the gate.

"But that's impossible!" Mom cried, raising her hands to her cheeks. "They can't lock people inside an amusement park!"

"Maybe it's another joke," Luke suggested. "Everything in this place turns out to be a joke. Maybe this is one, too."

I lifted the heavy padlock again. "It doesn't look like a joke, Luke," I said unhappily.

"Then there must be another gate where they want us to exit," Mom suggested.

"Maybe," Dad said doubtfully. "Maybe there's a side exit. But I haven't seen one."

"What are we going to do?" Clay asked, whining. His face was red, and he was breathing hard.

"Where *is* everyone?" Luke demanded, whining, too. "They've got to let us leave. They've *got* to!"

"Let's try to stay calm," Dad said, putting a hand on Luke's shoulder. "There's no reason to panic. This is a strange place, but we're not in any danger."

"He's right," Mom broke in. "There's no reason to be afraid. We'll be out of here and on our way home in no time." She forced a smile.

"As soon as we get out, I'll buy you guys pizzas and big, cold drinks," Dad promised. "And we'll all have a good laugh about our terrifying adventures today in HorrorLand."

"But how do we get out?" Luke demanded shrilly.

"Well . . ." Dad rubbed his chin.

"Do you think we could climb the fence?" I asked.

We all raised our eyes to the top of the iron fence. It was way over our heads. It must have been about twenty feet tall.

"I can't climb that!" Clay cried. "I'd fall!"

"It's too high," Mom said quickly.

"Bad idea," I murmured.

A large white cloud drifted over the sun. Our shadows grew longer over the pavement. The air quickly grew cooler.

I felt a chill run down my back.

"There's *got* to be a way out of this stupid park!" I cried angrily. I hoisted up the padlock and slammed it against the bars of the gate.

"Hold on, Lizzy," Dad said soothingly. "We just have to find one of those costumed park workers. They'll tell us how to get out."

"Uh . . . Dad . . ." I turned and saw Luke grab Dad's arm. "Here they come."

We all uttered astonished cries as we saw the Horrors crossing the plaza. Dozens of them. They moved quickly, with a steady rhythm. Silently.

A few seconds before, the plaza had been empty. Now it was filled with green-costumed Horrors marching toward us, spreading out, preparing to surround us.

I could feel the panic rise up from my stomach. My knees began to shake. I stared in horror at them as they drew closer, closer. I couldn't speak. I couldn't move.

"What are they going to *do*?" Clay cried, his features twisted in terror. He slipped behind Dad. "What are they going to do to us?" he cried.

22

We huddled together as the Horrors marched silently toward us. The only sound was the soft *thud* of their monster feet on the pavement, and their long purple tails dragging on the ground.

"There are *hundreds* of them!" Mom murmured. She grabbed Dad's arm with one hand. She slipped her other arm around my shoulders and pulled me closer.

We had our backs against the iron fence. We stared helplessly at the grinning, green faces, the bulging yellow eyes, which appeared to be laughing cruelly at us.

Finally, they stopped a few feet in front of us.

The plaza was still and silent. Terrifyingly silent.

The sun was still hidden behind the big cloud. Two large, black birds swooped low in the gray sky.

We stared at the Horrors, and they stared back at us.

I swallowed hard, leaning against my mother. I could feel her entire body trembling.

I took a deep breath and then cried out: "What do you want?" The sound of my own voice startled me.

One of the Horrors, a young woman, stepped forward.

Frightened, I tried to back up. But my back was already pressed against the fence.

"What do you want?" I repeated in a trembling voice.

The costumed Horror stared at us one by one. "I want to thank you," she said in a cheery voice.

"Huh?" I uttered.

"I'm the HorrorLand MC. We all want to thank you for being our guests today." She flashed us a warm smile.

"You mean we can *go*?" Luke demanded, half-hidden behind my dad.

"Of course," the Horror said, grinning warmly. "But first we all want to thank you for appearing on *HorrorLand Hidden Camera*."

The dozens of Horrors behind her broke into applause and loud cheers.

"Huh? You mean this is some kind of show?" Dad demanded, frowning.

"See the cameras?" the MC asked. She gestured up to two tall poles in the plaza.

Raising my eyes to the top, I saw two TV cameras.

"You mean we were on TV?" Luke cried.

"Since the moment you arrived," the MC replied. "Our hidden cameras followed you everywhere. From the hilarious scene where we blew up your car, our cameras were with you. And I know our home audience *loved* the terrified expressions on your faces and all of your horrified screams as you took our HorrorLand rides!"

"Now, wait a minute," Dad said angrily. He took a step forward. His hands were balled into tense fists at his sides. "You say this is a TV show? How come I've never seen it?"

"We're seen every weekend on The Monster Channel," the Horror replied.

"Oh," Dad replied quickly, lowering his eyes. "We don't have cable."

"You should get it," the Horror told him. "You're missing a lot of great, scary shows on The Monster Channel."

The Horrors all clapped and cheered.

"Well, you've been very good sports," the MC continued, her yellow eyes bouncing in front of her head as she talked. "We've enjoyed having you. And to show our appreciation, we have a brand-new car waiting for you in the parking lot!"

More cheers and applause from the Horrors.

"A new car? That's excellent!" Luke exclaimed.

"Does that mean we can leave?" Clay asked timidly.

The Horror nodded. "Yes, it's time for you to leave. The real exit is right over there, through that doorway."

She pointed to a tall, green building near the end of the fence. I saw a yellow door on the side.

"Take the yellow door," the Horror instructed. "And thanks again for appearing on *HorrorLand Hidden Camera!*"

As all the Horrors clapped their big, green hands, we stepped away from the fence and hurried toward the exit. "I can't believe we were on TV the whole time!" Mom declared.

"And we're getting a new car!" Luke exclaimed happily. He started jumping up and down. Then he leaped onto Clay's back, nearly knocking him over.

I laughed. It was good to see the old Luke back with us.

"We've got to get cable!" Luke told Dad. "I want to see The Monster Channel. It's *got* to be awesome!"

"We'll have to order it so we can see ourselves," Mom said.

I reached the yellow door first and pulled it open. I stepped into an enormous room, with white walls that shone under the bright white lights from the ceiling.

"Is *this* the exit?" I cried.

As soon as we were all inside, the door slammed shut with a *bang* that made my heart skip.

Then all the lights went out.

"Welcome to the HorrorLand Challenge!" boomed a deep, frightening voice over a loudspeaker.

"Huh?" I gazed blindly around, trying to see something — anything — in the total darkness.

"You have one minute to go through the Monster Obstacle Course," the voice thundered. "Please keep in mind that the games are now over. This is real. You're playing for your life!"

23

"We've been tricked!" I heard Dad cry angrily. And then he shouted at the top of his lungs, *"Let's get out of here!"*

"Run!" the deep voice boomed over the loudspeaker. "You have fifty-six seconds."

Dad started to shout again. But we stopped when a dim light came up, and a disgusting four-armed creature stepped toward us.

"Ohhh!" I cried out without even realizing it.

The size of a gorilla, the monster had huge green eyes surrounded by thick red fur over its face. Saliva drooled from its mouth. And as it opened its jaws wider, two rows of long fangs slid over its thin purple lips.

"Don't just stand there! Run! This is an obstacle course!" the voice boomed impatiently. "You have fifty seconds to live! At least make a good race of it!"

The monster uttered a low growl and lumbered toward us in the dim light. Its jaws were opened wide as if preparing to bite. Its four enormous, clawed hands swiped at the air in front of it.

I was too stunned to move, too frightened to run.

But, suddenly, I felt a hand grab mine and tug me hard.

It was Dad, I realized, trying to pull me to safety.

I heard the boys screaming in fear. I felt Mom brush beside me as we started to stumble forward.

"Run! Run!" the deep voice urged over the shrieks of the two boys.

I couldn't see where I was running. The light was so dim, so shadowy. I saw only a blur now, a blur of running feet, of moving shadows.

The monster let out a deafening roar. I covered my ears and kept running.

Its four clawed hands swiped at Dad. Missed.

We hurtled past it.

Only to face two giant birds, at least ten feet tall. They looked like cranes. They squawked and flapped their enormous wings. It sounded like canvas tents flapping in a strong wind.

"Ohh! Help!"

Was that *me* shrieking like that?

Was I really being wrapped in their hot, flapping wings? Smothered? Choked?

"No — *please!*"

How did I break away?

Was I being chased now by six growling piglike creatures with sharp, pointed teeth curling from their twisted mouths?

The screams and terrified shrieks of my family rose over the beating birds' wings, the monstrous growls and grunts.

I heard Dad cry out. And in the dim light, I saw him struggling to free himself from the four-armed creature.

"No!" I screamed as I felt something warm wrap around my ankle. A fur-covered snake!

I screamed again and kicked wildly, sending it flying into the darkness.

But before I could move away, another furry snake spun around my leg, tightening quickly.

I bent and pulled at it as it hissed in protest.

I tossed it aside.

"Run! Run!" the voice on the loudspeaker boomed. "Twenty seconds to live!"

More monsters loomed in front of us. Disgusting yellow lizardlike creatures with dark, flicking tongues like bullwhips. A hopping furry ball that roared as it hopped, sharp teeth poking out of three mouths.

Hissing snakes, enormous, buzzing insects with glowing red eyes, more grunting pig monsters. Then a giant bearlike creature came at us on two legs. It tossed its dark, round head back, and laughed like a hyena as its paws punched the air.

"Help me!" I heard Luke shriek. And then I saw him disappear, wrapped inside the beating wings of one of the giant birds.

The bird *cawed* in triumph as its wings tightened around my brother.

"Ten seconds!" the voice boomed.

"No!" I cried. I lunged toward the bird, grasped the beating wing, and pulled it open.

Luke slid out, and we both began to run.

Monsters growled, and flapped, and grunted, and roared.

"Are we . . . going to make it?" Luke asked in a tiny voice.

I didn't have a chance to answer.

Two powerful paws grabbed me around the waist, hoisted me high in the air, then slammed me to the floor.

I landed hard on my stomach. My forehead hit the floor.

Dizzy and hurt, I looked up in time to see an enormous, elephantlike creature about to flatten me with its huge, furry back foot.

I'm not going to make it, I realized.

I'm not going to make it.

24

The enormous, flat foot lowered over me slowly, steadily. The monster was taking its time.

It all seemed to be happening in slow motion.

I wanted to move. I wanted to roll out from under it.

But the fall had taken my breath away. I lay there gasping, watching the monster foot coming down to crush me.

"Ohhh." I couldn't catch my breath. I couldn't squirm away.

I could feel the heat of the monster foot. I could smell its putrid sweat.

The foot pressed down on my stomach.

I shut my eyes and waited for the pain.

The jarring blast of a buzzer made my eyes shoot open.

The buzz echoed through the vast room.

The monster raised its heavy foot from my body. The floor shook under its weight as it began to lumber away.

Am I alive? I wondered.

Or am I only dreaming that I'm still alive?

Is that creature really leaving without crushing me?

The buzzer echoed in my ear. Then it abruptly stopped. The loudspeaker crackled on.

"Time's up!" a woman's voice said. The voice of the HorrorLand MC who had led us to this terrifying obstacle course.

"Time is up. What a thrilling race!" she gushed.

I groaned and started to pull myself up. In the dim light, I saw that all of the monsters had vanished.

"That was a tough battle," the MC continued over the loudspeaker. "Do we have any survivors?"

"Yes, we do," the deep, booming voice replied.

"How many survivors do we have in there?" the woman asked.

"Three," the booming voice replied. "Three survivors out of five."

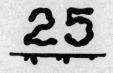

25

A cold chill ran down my body.

I opened my mouth in a silent cry of shock and leaped to my feet.

Three out of five?

Did that mean that two of us were dead?

My chest still ached. My knees were trembling. I squinted into the dim light, searching desperately for the others.

Halfway across the room, I saw Luke and Clay. They were huddled together, walking as if in a daze toward the far wall.

"Hey — !" I tried to call to them. But my voice came out a choked whisper.

Where were Mom and Dad?

Were they both killed by the monsters?

Three out of five. Three out of five.

"Nooooooooo!" I finally found my voice and let out a horrified wail that echoed off the walls.

"Excuse me. A slight mistake," the deep voice boomed. "Make that five out of five survivors."

"Five out of five!" the HorrorLand MC exclaimed. "A new record. We've never had a perfect score before. Let's give them a round of applause, everyone!"

I took a deep breath and held it, trying to stop my trembling.

They're okay! I thought happily. Mom and Dad are okay.

And then I saw them. They had their arms around Luke and Clay and were making their way toward me.

"We're okay!" I cried, rushing to them, my arms outstretched. "We're okay!"

All five of us huddled in the center of the dark room, hugging each other and sobbing.

Dad's arm was bleeding from a deep gash. One of the monsters had clawed him.

Aside from that, we were shaken but not hurt.

"Now what?" Luke asked in a trembling voice. "Are they going to let us go?"

"They can't get away with this," Dad said angrily. "They can't do this to people and get away with it. I don't care if it *is* TV!"

"Those monsters were real!" I exclaimed with a shudder. "It wasn't a fake. They were really trying to kill us."

"How do we get out?" Luke demanded. "Will they let us out?"

We all started chattering at once, our voices high and frightened.

Suddenly, the ceiling lights flashed on, flooding the room with bright light. And the MC's voice broke through our frightened conversation. "Let's bring our winners out with a round of applause!" she announced cheerfully.

We all cried out as the floor began to tilt beneath us. I grabbed on to Dad, and we started to slide.

The floor tilted down like a sliding board. And we slid out of the room — and landed in the plaza outside.

Still feeling dazed, I jumped quickly to my feet as the HorrorLand MC hurried to greet us. The big crowd of Horrors behind her was clapping and cheering.

"You can't do this to us!" I screeched.

I was so angry, I didn't know what I was doing. I just totally freaked.

I leaped at the woman, grabbed the top of her mask, and started to pull it off with both hands.

"You can't do this! You can't!" I shrieked. "Let me see your face! Let me see who you really are!"

Using all of my strength, I gave the mask a hard tug.

Then I screamed and let go as I realized the truth.

26

She wasn't wearing a mask!

The monstrous green face was *her* face.

She wasn't wearing a monster costume. None of the Horrors were wearing costumes, I realized.

I stepped back, raising my hands in horror as if trying to shield myself. "You — you're really monsters!" I stammered.

They nodded back at me, pleased grins on their ugly faces. Their yellow eyes bobbed gleefully.

"You — you're all monsters!" I screamed. "But — but you said this was a TV show," I stammered to the Horror MC.

Her bulging yellow eyes gazed at me. "We're happy to say it is the top-rated show on The Monster Channel," she said cheerily. "Thanks to great contestants like you and your family. The Monster Channel is watched by nearly two million monsters all over the world."

"But — but — " I stammered, taking another step back.

"People don't always take us seriously," she continued. "People come to HorrorLand and think it's all a big joke. People laugh at the signs around the park. They laugh at the rides and attractions. But it's all very serious to us. All of it."

My father stepped up beside me, shaking a fist angrily. "But you can't do this to innocent people!" he shouted. "You can't bring people into this park to torture them, and — and — "

"Oh, I'm sorry. Our time is up for this week," the MC interrupted, shaking her enormous green head. "I'm sad to say it's time to say good-bye to our special guests for this week."

"Now, wait — " Dad shouted, raising both hands for quiet.

The crowd of Horrors silently pushed forward. We had no choice but to start moving with them.

"Let me show you people the way we say good-bye on *The HorrorLand Hidden Camera Show*," the MC said.

Dad tried to hold back, to resist, but several Horrors bumped against him. They were bumping all of us now, pushing us toward what appeared to be a round, purple pond just beyond the plaza.

We couldn't fight back. There were too many of them.

We couldn't run. They had us surrounded.

They drove us like sheepdogs herding cattle. In a few seconds, we were standing on the edge of the purple pond.

A foul smell rose up from the pond. The purple liquid bubbled and gurgled, making a sick sucking sound.

"Let us go!" Luke cried shrilly. "We want to go home!"

The HorrorLand MC ignored his frantic pleas and stepped to the edge of the gurgling pond. "Saying good-bye is always sad," she said. "So we try to have a little fun with our farewells."

"Just let us go!" Luke insisted. Dad put a hand on his shoulder to try to comfort him.

We all stared at the MC as she raised a large rock in one hand and held it over the disgusting, bubbling pond. "Watch," she instructed us with a smile.

She let the rock drop into the pond.

As soon as it touched the thick surface, it was pulled down with a loud sucking sound.

"See how easy it is to say good-bye?" the Horror said, turning to us. "Now, will you jump in — or do you want to be pushed?"

27

Silently, the Horrors began moving in on us. Closer. Closer.

Backing up, Clay tripped over my foot and nearly fell into the gurgling purple pit. I grabbed him and held on to him until he regained his balance.

All five of us were standing on the edge of the pit.

The sour odor swept over me. I felt sick. The thick, purple slime lapped up at my ankles as if reaching out to grab me.

"Mom! Dad — !" I cried. I didn't know what I expected them to do. We were all helpless.

I knew we weren't going to escape this time.

Without realizing it, we were all holding hands.

"Will you jump in — or do you want to be pushed?" The MC repeated her question.

"I'm real sorry," Dad murmured to us, ignoring her. "I'm real sorry I brought you here. I — I didn't know . . ." His voice broke. He lowered his eyes.

"Dad, it's not your fault!" I told him, squeezing his hand.

And as I squeezed his hand, I had an idea.

A wild idea. A stupid idea. A really crazy idea.

I knew I had to try it. It was the only idea I had.

"People laugh at everything in the park," the HorrorLand MC had told us. *"But it's all very serious to us,"* she'd said.

All very serious . . .

Very serious . . .

She stood right in front of me now, waiting for us to jump to our deaths, eager for us to get sucked down into the purple slime.

I knew this was my last chance. I knew it was crazy.

But I knew I had to try it.

I stepped up to the MC, reached out, and pinched her arm as hard as I could.

28

Her mouth opened wide, and she let out a startled gasp.

She tried to pull her arm away. But I held on and pinched harder. "The Mad Pincher strikes again!" I shouted, remembering Luke's annoying cry.

Her yellow eyes rolled around crazily. "No!" she pleaded.

Harder. Harder.

And then I was the one to cry out as her mouth opened wide, and, with a loud *whoosh*, a rush of air escaped her lips.

I leaped back.

As the air rushed from her mouth, she appeared to deflate, just like a balloon.

I gaped in amazement as she folded helplessly to the ground.

An angry cry rose up from the crowd of Horrors. "Inflate her!" one of them yelled. "Inflate her immediately!"

They began moving in on us, growling and grumbling menacingly.

"Pinch them!" I shouted to my family. "Pinch them! The *'No Pinching'* signs that we thought were so stupid — they were serious! The Horrors deflate if they're pinched!"

A Horror stepped up, arms outstretched to push me into the pond. I pinched his arm hard, and a few seconds later, he deflated.

I heard the *whoosh* of air escaping to my right, and saw that Luke had deflated one, too.

Whoosh! Another one deflated and folded to the pavement.

That's all it took.

The plaza filled with frightened cries and gasps of horror.

The alarmed Horrors turned and ran. *Stampeded* is a better word. They scattered through the park, screaming as they ran.

Taking a long, deep breath, I happily watched them flee. "See? I always come through in a pinch!" I said, amazing myself by making a joke.

I don't think anyone else in my family heard me. They were shouting for joy, hugging each other, jumping up and down.

"Let's get out of here!" I shouted. I started running toward the front gate. The others followed close behind.

The gate was open now. I guess the Horrors

had opened it, figuring the only place we were heading was to the bottom of the purple pond.

Without looking back, we ran out onto the empty parking lot.

And stopped.

"No car," I murmured.

In all the excitement, I had forgotten that our car had been blown up.

I let out a weary sigh. I felt as if I were deflating, just like the Horrors. "Now what?" I asked, staring across the enormous, flat parking lot.

"It's too far to walk!" Luke wailed. "How do we get out of here?"

"The buses!" Mom cried, pointing. I turned my eyes to the row of purple-and-green buses parked on the side of the lot. They glowed under the bright afternoon sun.

"Yeah!" Dad cried excitedly. "Maybe we can start one up and get away from here!"

We started jogging over the pavement to the buses. "Cross your fingers," Dad called, leading the way. "Maybe they leave the keys in them. It's our only chance!"

"Hurry!" Luke shouted suddenly. "They're coming!"

My heart leaped in my chest. I turned back toward the gate.

Sure enough, the Horrors were pouring out of

the park, chasing after us. "Give up! You cannot escape!" one of them screamed.

"No one ever escapes!" another Horror shouted.

"Hurry!" Luke cried. "Hurry! They're going to catch us!"

29

With the Horrors close behind, shouting and threatening us, we ran full speed toward the row of buses.

My heart was pounding almost as loud as my sneakers against the pavement. My throat ached, and I had a sharp pain in my side.

But I kept running.

"You cannot escape!"

"Stop now!"

"Give up!"

The angry cries of the Horrors sounded even closer. But I didn't turn back to see if they were catching up.

The door to the first bus was open. Dad got there first and scrambled up the steps and inside.

Mom stepped in, followed by the two boys.

The engine coughed, then started up with a roar as I pulled myself inside. The bus door slid shut behind me. "Dad — the keys!" I choked out.

"Yes! They're here!" he cried happily. "Hold on! We're getting away!"

He lowered his foot on the gas pedal, and the bus shot forward. I stumbled down the aisle and fell into a seat behind Luke and Clay.

"Hurry! They're coming! They're coming!" Luke and Clay were screaming in unison.

I could hear the angry shouts of the Horrors through the closed bus windows.

"We're okay!" Dad cried, leaning over the big steering wheel. "We're okay! We're *outta* here!"

"Yes!" I shouted happily. "Yes!"

We all started to cheer. We kept cheering until we were out of the parking lot and back on the highway.

We laughed and celebrated all the way home.

The drive took hours and hours, but we didn't care. We were safe! We had escaped!

It was night when Dad pulled the bus up our driveway. "Home, sweet home!" I cried joyfully.

We all piled eagerly out of the bus. I took a deep breath and stretched. The air smelled so sweet and fresh. A full moon made the front lawn shine.

Then I saw him. It was a Horror, and he was clinging to the back of our bus. "Oh, no!" I cried out.

"What are you doing there?" Dad demanded.

"Did you ride back there the whole way home?" Luke asked in disbelief.

I shrank back as the Horror let go of the bus and slid to the ground. His yellow eyes studied us menacingly. He moved toward us quickly.

Clay and Luke hid behind Dad. Mom's mouth dropped open in fright.

"What do you *want*?" I cried.

He reached out his green hand. "Here," he said. "We forgot to give you your free passes for next year!"

Add *more*

Goosebumps

to your collection . . .
A chilling preview of
what's next from
R.L. STINE

WHY I'M AFRAID
OF BEES

7

I spent the next few days changing my Band-Aids and hoping the woman from Person-to-Person Vacations would call me.

At first, I ran to answer the phone every time it rang. But of course it was never for me. Usually, it was one of Krissy's dumb friends, wanting to giggle and gossip.

One afternoon, I was reading a science-fiction book in my usual spot behind the big maple tree. I heard a sound, and peered around from behind the tree.

Sure enough, there was Mr. Andretti walking across the lawn. He was dressed in his beekeeping outfit. As I watched, Mr. Andretti went to the screened-in area off the garage and started opening up the little doors to his beehives.

Bzzzzzz.

I covered my ears, but I couldn't shut out the loud, droning hum. How I hated that sound! It was just so frightening.

I shivered and decided it was time to go back inside.

As I climbed to my feet, a bullet-sized object shot right by my nose. A bee!

Were the bees escaping for real this time?

I gasped and stared over at Andretti's house. Then I almost choked. There *was* a big hole in the screen around the beekeeping area.

A *lot* of bees were flying out!

"Ow!" I cried out as a bee landed on the side of my head and buzzed loudly into my ear.

Frantically, I batted it away. Then I ran toward the house. For one wild moment, I thought about calling the police or maybe the paramedics.

But as I slammed the back door, I heard an all-too-familiar sound. "Haw haw haw!"

Once again, Mr. Andretti was laughing at me.

I pounded my fist into my other hand. Oh, how I'd like to sock that guy in the nose! I thought.

I was interrupted by the sound of the phone ringing.

"Give me a break!" I cried as I stomped off to answer it. "Don't Krissy's moron friends have anything better to do than talk on the phone all day long?"

"Whaddya want?" I snarled into the mouthpiece.

"Is this Gary?" a woman's voice asked. "Gary Lutz?"

"Uh . . . yes," I answered in surprise. "I'm Gary."

"Hi, Gary. This is Ms. Karmen. From Person-to-Person Vacations? Remember me?"

My heart started thumping in my chest. "Yes. I remember," I answered.

"Well, if you're still interested, we've found a match for you!"

"A match?"

"Correct," said Ms. Karmen. "We've found a boy who wants to switch bodies with you for a week. Are you interested?"

I hesitated for a few seconds. But, then, as I gazed out the back door of the kitchen, I saw a big, fat bee throwing itself against the outside of our screen door. "Haw haw!" Mr. Andretti's scornful laughter boomed across the back yard.

My mouth tightened into a thin line. "Yes," I said firmly. "I'm really interested. When can we make the switch?"

"Why, we could do it now," said Ms. Karmen. "If that's all right with you."

My pulse raced as I thought. My parents were both out for the afternoon, and Krissy was playing at a friend's house. The timing was perfect. I'd never get another chance like this!

"Now is great!" I exclaimed.

"Terrific, Gary. It will take me about twenty minutes to get to your house."

"I'll be waiting."

The next twenty minutes seemed to take forever. While I waited, I paced back and forth in the living room, wondering what my new body would be like.

What would my new parents be like? My house? My clothes? Would I actually have some friends this time around?

By the time Ms. Karmen arrived, I was a wreck. When the doorbell rang, my hand was sweating so much, I could barely turn the doorknob to let her in.

"Let's go in the kitchen," Ms. Karmen suggested. "I like to set up my equipment on a table." She opened a small case and took out some black boxes with monitors on them.

I showed her the way to the kitchen. "So who's this kid who wants to switch places with me?" I asked.

"His name is Dirk Davis."

Dirk Davis! I thought excitedly. Even his name sounded cool. "What does he look like?"

Ms. Karmen opened up a white photo album. "Here's his picture," she said, passing it to me.

I looked down at a picture of a tall, athletic-looking blond boy in black Lycra bike shorts and a blue muscle shirt. I blinked in surprise.

"He looks like a surfer or something!" I cried. "Why in the world does he want to switch bodies with me? Is this some kind of trick?"

Ms. Karmen smiled. "Well, to be honest, it's not exactly your *body* he's interested in, Gary. He wants your *mind*. You see, Dirk needs someone who is good in math. He has some very hard math tests coming up in summer school. He wants you to take them for him."

"Oh," I said. I felt relieved. "Well, I usually do pretty well on math tests."

"We know that, Gary. Person-to-Person does its homework. You're very good at math. Dirk's good at skateboarding."

I sat down at the table.

Bzzzzzz.

A bee buzzed right under my nose. "Hey!" I yelled, jumping back up. "How'd that bee get in here?"

Ms. Karmen glanced up from her equipment. "Your back door is open just a bit. Now please sit down and try to relax. I need to fasten this strap around your wrist."

With a nervous glance at the back door, I sat back down. Ms. Karmen strapped a black band around my wrist. Then she started fiddling with some wires attached to one of her machines.

Bzzzzzz.

Another bee flew in front of me, and I wiggled around in my chair.

"Please sit still, Gary. Otherwise the equipment won't work."

"Who can sit still with all these bees buzzing around in here?" I asked. I lowered my eyes and saw three fat bees walking across the table.

Bzzzzzz.

Another bee flew past my right eye.

"What's up with these bees?" I was starting to panic.

"Don't pay any attention to them," Ms. Karmen said, "and they won't bother you." She made one more adjustment to her machine. "Besides, Dirk Davis isn't afraid of bees. And, as soon as I flip this switch, you won't be, either!"

"But . . . !"

ZZAAAAPPPP!

A blinding white light flashed in front of my eyes.

I tried to cry out.

But my breath caught in my throat.

The light grew brighter, brighter.

And then I sank into a deep pool of blackness.

8

Something was wrong.

Colors returned. But they were a total blur.

I struggled to make everything come clear. But I couldn't seem to focus on anything.

My new body didn't feel right, either. I was lying on my back, and I felt light as a feather, light enough to float away.

Could this be Dirk Davis's tall, muscular body? It certainly didn't feel like it!

Was this some kind of trick! I asked myself. Was the picture of Dirk Davis a phony? Was he really a lot smaller than he looked in the photo album?

I reached out one of my hands and tried to touch my stomach. But my hand felt really weird, too. It was small, and my arm seemed to be bending in several places at once!

What's going on? I wondered, trembling with fright.

Why do I feel so *weird*?

"Whooooa!" I cried out as I finally managed to touch my body. "Yuck." My skin was soft. And it was covered with a fine layer of fuzz.

"Help! Ms. Karmen! Help! Something's wrong!" I tried to shout.

But there was something wrong with my voice. It came out all tiny and squeaky. Little mouse squeaks.

I rolled over onto my stomach and tried to get up. I spread my arms to balance myself.

I gasped as I realized my feet weren't even touching the ground!

I was flying!

"What's happening to me?" I cried in my squeaky little voice. I floated forward and crashed into a kitchen cupboard.

"Ow! Help me!"

I moved my strange new arms and realized I had some control over which way I flew. I felt some weird muscles in my back going into action. Testing my new muscles, I flew over to the kitchen window.

Exhausted, I landed on the sill. I turned my head to one side. Then I gasped in fright.

A hideous monster was reflected in the window glass!

The creature had two huge glaring eyes. And it was staring right at me.

I tried to scream. But I was too terrified to utter a sound.

I — I have to get away! I decided.

I moved my feet and started to run. The monster in the glass ran, too.

I stopped and stared at the window glass. The monster stopped and stared back at me.

"Oh, no! Please — no!" I cried. "Please don't let it be true!" I reached up and tried to cover my eyes. The creature in the window did the same thing.

And suddenly I knew the hideous truth. The monster in the mirror — it was me.

Ms. Karmen had messed up. Totally.

And now I was trapped inside the body of a bee!

About the Author

R.L. STINE is the author of over two dozen best-selling thrillers and mysteries for young people. Recent titles for teenagers include *The Hitchhiker*, *Halloween Night*, *The Dead Girlfriend*, and *The Baby-sitter III*, all published by Scholastic. He is also the author of the *Fear Street* series.

When he isn't writing scary books, he is head writer of the children's TV show *Eureeka's Castle*, seen on Nickelodeon.

Bob lives in New York City with his wife, Jane, and thirteen-year-old son, Matt.

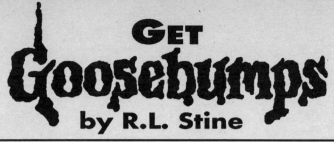